THE LUCKIEST KID IN THE WORLD

DANNY WALLACE

Illustrated by *gemma* CORRELL

SIMON & SCHUSTER

First published in Great Britain in 2022 by Simon & Schuster UK Ltd

Text copyright © 2022 Danny Wallace
Illustrations copyright © 2022 Gemma Correll

1 3 5 7 9 10 8 6 4 2

Simon & Schuster UK Ltd
1st Floor, 222 Gray's Inn Road
London
WC1X 8HB

www.simonandschuster.co.uk
www.simonandschuster.com.au
www.simonandschuster.co.in

Simon & Schuster Australia, Sydney
Simon & Schuster India, New Delhi

A CIP catalogue record for this book is available from the British Library.

PB ISBN 978-1-4711-9689-8
eBook ISBN 978-1-4711-9690-4
eAudio ISBN 978-1-3985-0337-3

Typeset in the UK by Sorrel Packham

Printed and bound by CPI Group (UK) Ltd, Croydon, CR0 4YY

MIX
Paper from
responsible sources
FSC® C171272

For my dad,
who made me the
luckiest kid in the world.

CHAPTER ONE

This is the first time I have ever told anyone the WHOLE story, so I hope I'm doing it right.

I bet you already know who I am because I became very famous this year. Maybe even the most famous boy in town.

And, if you've heard all about me and the strangest two weeks ever, you'll probably be wondering why I did what I did.

I mean – what kid would DO that?
A kid who's OUT OF HIS MIND?!

So, anyway, it's this completely normal Thursday evening and Mum's already walked into my room like three times to make sure I'm working on my school project. I've been researching it all week, and it's all about what makes THE MODERN FAMILY.

We have to compare our family to families of the past, when everyone had a horse and cart or lived in a chimney or whatnot.

AVERAGE-
SIZED
RABBIT

In the past, everybody was much smaller, like the size of a rabbit, I think, and they had names like 'Forsooth!' and 'Hamlet'.

My name is Joe and I am not

the size of a rabbit – I am average ten-year-old-kid size.

As I'm sure you know, I live in Didcot, which used to have a big power station, but now doesn't, and also has a lot of people who used to work at the power station, but now don't.

Didcot is famous because in the 1800s William Bradbery was the first person in Britain to sell watercress.

But enough of the important stuff; let's get back to my family.

AVERAGE-SIZED TEN-YEAR-OLD

So my dad is five foot nine inches (175.259 cm!) tall, which is the size of seven and a half rabbits.

He is thirty-nine and has size nine feet and works in an

office. Once a day he will remind us he used to be in a rock band called Samurai!, who played two gigs in 1996. One was at his school, and the other was in the local old people's home, where they were immediately told to leave because no one had asked them to be there.

So Dad gave up being a rock star so he could follow his dream of working in an office all day every day. He sold his guitar and Mum says he's never been the same since. He is a great dad who never puts any pressure on me to be the best at anything. 'That's good enough for me, Joe!' he says sometimes. Though secretly I think that kind of attitude is why Samurai! never played a third gig.

My mum? She is five foot seven inches tall (170.18 cm!) and she drives a grey Ford Fiesta, which she bought when she turned forty and sold her old camper van.

Mum is like a lot of mums or dads in that when anyone

asks if she's a good cook, she always says: 'I make a mean Bolognese!'

Mum's trick is that she adds three dots of chilli sauce, and she once had this crazy idea that she could sell her spaghetti Bolognese from her camper van. But, after talking a lot with Dad, I think she realised that people in Didcot could make spaghetti on their own at home and add three dots of chilli sauce with very little bother, and also they would prefer not buying it out of a van. So now Mum works in an office like Dad. Working in an office is very much the family trade and I expect one day I will work in an office too.

Hundreds of years ago, families would be made up of one or two parents and around 350 children, who would all live in a small house with one bedroom next to a factory. They would all have to share one telly, I think, and very often lots of them would die from not having any windows or because the bed was too small or from soot or something.

I am lucky because I have my own bedroom and, thank goodness, my little sister, Mickey, has her own bedroom too, but poor Mum and Dad have to share one.

Sometimes, after school, I get to go to Nico's Café on the high street, where Nico makes me two boiled eggs on toast while Mum takes Mickey to Robo Dance or Boogie Ballet. Mum says two boiled eggs are cheaper than a childminder. Don't get me wrong, I also like burgers and hot dogs, but somehow Nico makes the best two boiled eggs on toast in Didcot. And, on his seventieth birthday last year, he made *me* a cake to celebrate!

I am usually the only person in there, and definitely the only one who orders two boiled eggs on toast, so Nico has time to tell me stories about Italy. Famous Italians include the Mario Brothers and a boxer called Rocky.

I am trying to grow a moustache like Nico, but I am ten and it is slow-going. Knowing my luck, Mickey will grow one before me, even though she is six and a girl and totally obsessed with pandas. Mum and Mickey's teachers think everything Mickey does is amazing and they keep telling her she is 'so advanced'. She could throw a pencil against the wall and everybody would applaud – seriously! But I can come top twenty in whatever video game I'm playing *and* level up with a ton of XP, and

everybody just tells me that's 'nice' and could I please not call them at work about this stuff.

So, anyway, I was trying to think of what to write about my family and I was starting to realise there wasn't much to write about, apart from my sister always asking me to play and following me about all the time. But who wants to read that? That's why I put in the watercress thing I told you, and the bit about Nico's moustache.

But then just before bed I look out of my window, and I see this van parked outside. And it's got these three people in the front with clipboards. And they're all looking up at my window.

So, obviously, I think it must be the gas board or something. It doesn't even occur to me that my life is just twelve hours away from completely changing for ever.

CHAPTER TWO

My dad sets his alarm for 6.47 a.m. every day so that he can hit the snooze button for twenty-five minutes. That means that every five minutes from 6.47 a.m. to 7.12 a.m. the whole house has to hear *BAAAAH! BAAAAH! BAAAAH!* from the really aggressive alarm clock he bought at the market because it was cheap.

My street is a friendly street where the

people all do what I call 'street humour'.

This is when people make a joke about something not very funny.

So, if you see someone washing their car, you have to say, 'You can do mine next!' and then you both do a big laugh.

Or, if you see someone cutting their grass, you have to say, 'You can do mine next!' and then you both do a big laugh.

It means someone on our street is always laughing, which I suppose is better than screaming.

Anyway, as I'm lying in bed, I can hear a few people laughing outside. Maybe someone tripped over and someone else said, 'Enjoy your trip!'

'Another day, another dollar!' shouts Mickey, bursting into my room.

She's shouting this because when Dad gets up every day he usually says, 'Another day, another dollar!' even though he is paid in pounds and has never even been to America.

But today we hear him say, 'Who are all those people outside our house?'

* * *

Mum is peeking out of the front-door window when we get downstairs. Mum is someone who doesn't like a lot of fuss, and she senses that soon there might be a lot of fuss.

That van is still outside and now there are even more people. Some of them are wearing headsets like Beyoncé and someone must have called the news because there's a TV camera. The mechanic at number fourteen is pretending to work on his car, but really he's staring at our house. The artist at number twenty-two is poking her face through the curtains. In fact, all the neighbours are watching our house in case there's been a scandal or something and now we're all going to jail.

'Did you pay that parking ticket?' asks Mum, and Dad says, 'Of course I did!'

We are generally a very law-abiding family.

Then we watch as a man with a microphone opens our front gate and starts to walk down the path, followed by the TV camera.

'Oh no,' says Mum. 'What do we do?'

The doorbell rings and then the man knocks twice on the door, really loudly.

'What do we do?' asks Mum again, taking a step back.

Dad takes a deep breath and says, 'I'll handle this!' and

he puffs out his chest and opens the door.

The man outside suddenly says, 'I'm Tony Dawson from *Good Morning and Wake Up!*'

He looks at us like we're supposed to know who he is, but we don't watch *Good Morning and Wake Up!* – we watch the other one.

'I'm looking for one Joe Smith!' says Tony Dawson.

Well, that's lucky because we've only got one. It's me.

We all stand there, stunned. Why are they looking for me?

Dad steps to one side and Mum shoves me forward, like a human sacrifice. I stand there, blinking, as the camera moves closer.

'Are you Joe Smith of Didcot?'

Well, we're in Didcot, aren't we? It's not like I sleep here and then go to my real home 200 miles away.

'Yes?' I say.

'Ten years old? Average height?'

'That's right,' I say.

'In a family of four?'

'Yes,' I say.

'And is that your mum's grey Ford Fiesta?'

'It is,' I say.

'Can I have a look in your fridge?'

Tony Dawson opened our fridge and kept holding up various items to the camera and saying, 'Yes!'

We all stayed out of his way because he seemed very determined and we still didn't know if we were in some kind of trouble or something.

But he'd hold up some ham and say, 'Sliced ham – yes!' Or, 'Cheese dunkers – yes!'

Then he ran up to my room and had a look at my stuff. He seemed delighted. Next he led me back out to the front garden in front of all the neighbours and started asking me all these weird questions.

'How many really close friends do you have?'

I count in my head. It doesn't take long. It's basically one – Joe 2.

'Are you ever picked first or last at football?'

I don't think either has ever happened.

'What do you have for your breakfast?'

'Cereal,' I say.

'What did you have for your tea last night?'

'I had meaty pasta.' We eat a lot of meaty pasta.

And then, when I'd said that, he turns to the camera.

'Ladies and gentlemen, after a month of travelling up and down the country, we have finally done it. We have found the average town, and we are on an average street, outside an average house, with a *very* average family.'

I notice Mum frown at that bit.

'From secretly studying them, I can tell you they go to bed at the average time, they get up at the average time, they eat the average things, they drive the most average car in the most average colour, and they have two children – one of whom is an averagely tall ten-year-old that I can absolutely assure you seems wonderfully average in every way.'

Oh!

'His average-height parents married at the average age,

work in the average jobs, earn the average amount of money and live a very, *very* average life.'

Dad puts his hands on his hips like he's cross, but he doesn't know what he wants to say or how to say it.

'Joe Smith,' says Tony Dawson, putting his hand on my shoulder, 'you are very special indeed.'

'Am I?' I say.

'You are very special,' he goes, 'because you are *not* special at all.'

He gives me a big smile, like that's brilliant, then turns to face the camera.

'Meet the country's *Most Average Child*!'

CHAPTER THREE

It was certainly a very unusual start to the day.

As Dad drives me and Mickey to school, he doesn't even put the radio on. Usually, we listen to that show everyone listens to, but now he's lost in thought. I can't work out what he's thinking. I keep asking him if what happened was good or bad, but it's like he can't quite decide.

He keeps muttering things like, 'There's nothing wrong with fitting in,' or, 'It's good to keep your head down,' or, 'It's not a crime to *not* stand out,' but it's as if he's telling *himself* all this stuff, not me.

Dad always tells me that I really remind him of himself at my age. He says, 'That's good enough for me, Joe!', but he also says people shouldn't tell their kids how amazing they are all the time. Dad says if every kid is told they're amazing at everything, they're all going to turn into grown-ups who think they're exceptional when actually they're just normal, and this will be the greatest disappointment of their lives. He says, with me and Mickey, he just wants to tell us when we've done a good job, rather than tell us we can do anything. He says that way it will be a nice surprise to all of us if we do something cool, like he almost did with Samurai!

After Tony Dawson's announcement, all the TV

people had packed up immediately and driven off. We asked them if they wanted a cup of tea or something, but they all said no. Tony Dawson gave me his autograph – which I did *not* ask for – and also hung a small silver medal round my neck with AVERAGE written on it.

'Average,' muttered Dad for the umpteenth time. He didn't seem over the moon about it.

I personally think we probably are quite average. After all, literally everything Tony Dawson had said was true, and he kept saying they'd done their research. They'd thought, *What if we could find the average kid?* and somehow they'd ended up with me. And I saw their point. I mean, if you really thought about it, what did me or my family actually do that stood out?

Dad says he watches all the most popular TV shows because if they're popular that means they're good, right?

Mum reads all the books that her websites tell her are the most popular ones.

Apart from Nico's Café, we go to all the same places all the other families go to eat. Mum and Dad even named me Joe when Joe was the most popular name to give to a boy. Don't take my word for it – you can ask my best friend, Joe 2. And so what?

'What did the man mean, saying you were average?' goes Mickey, from the back seat.

'Because I think the best way to get through school is just to keep your head down and not cause a fuss, Mickey,' I say. And I was basically trying to make Dad say, 'Well done, Joe!', but he's still lost in his own thoughts.

As soon as I get to school, I know something's up.

Some of the parents stop talking as soon as we pull up and they nudge their kids, who all stare at me.

I don't know what to do, so I act cool and sling my bag over my shoulder. But the bag swings right round and whacks Mickey in the face.

'Hi, Jon!' shouts Jessica Berry, and even though she gets my name wrong I don't care because that's Jessica Berry and Jessica Berry never talks to me. I don't know what to do with my hands so I readjust my bag strap, but somehow I get Mickey caught in it, and now her head is trapped underneath my armpit.

Everyone is still staring at me as I untangle her, then Joe 2 runs up.

(I call Joe 'Joe 2' because I'm Joe 1, but Joe 2 calls *me* Joe 2 because Joe 2 thinks *he's* Joe 1. But when we're together it gets too confusing so we just use words like 'dude'.)

'Dude!' says Joe 2. 'You're famous! Look at your medal!'

He reads it out, all proud of me.

'*Average*. Wow. You're *special*.'

'No, he's not, he's *average*,' comes a voice, and I know exactly whose voice it is because it's Darren Harper's voice.

'He's the *most* average,' says Joe 2, trying to defend me, 'so that makes him special.'

Then Darren Harper goes all smirky and stands really close to me; so close I can smell the cornflakes stuck in his teeth.

'Look at me,' he says. 'I'm taller than you, so that means I'm taller than average. I'm stronger than you, so I'm stronger than average. I'm better looking than you, so I'm better looking than average. I guess now we have proof I'm better than you in every way . . . *Average Joe.*'

A load of kids all laugh at that.

Darren Harper is an equal-opportunities bully in that he makes fun of everybody. But there's never been anything about me that really stuck out, so I've never had an actual nickname from him before. Not like Big Feet Freddy or Lazy Susan. And any time I *have* stuck out – like if I missed a goal at football or if I had new shoes on – Darren's been there to put me back in my place.

'Come on, dude,' says Joe 2. 'Let's go and make you some business cards or something! *"Joe Smith – Just Yer Average Kid!"*'

I'm grateful to Joe 2, but, as we leave together, I don't like the fact that the other kids are *still* laughing at what Darren said. It's not a nice feeling.

It almost makes me want to take my medal off.

Our school had an Ofsted report that said it 'requires improvement', so Mr Chesil, the head teacher, put a new carpet in the staffroom and now I think we're all good.

My teacher is Mrs Beatty and when me and Joe 2 want to talk about her in secret we call her 'B.T.' because that's like a code she can't crack.

She's obviously seen me on telly this morning because when we sit down she says, 'I saw you on TV this morning!'

I must blush a bit because then she says, 'You're blushing a bit.'

She really seems to want to talk about it though.

'So you had no idea they were coming?' she says.

'No,' I say, pleased she enjoyed it. 'They just appeared out of a van!'

'And so what did you win?'

I tell her I'm not quite sure what she means.

'Well, they go to all that effort to find you,' she says, 'then they call you the country's most average child . . . What's in it for you?'

Oh. I hadn't really thought about that.

'He got a fake medal!' shouts Darren Harper from the back of the class, laughing. 'It's not even real silver, miss. It's just tin or something!'

Shut up, Darren Harper!

'Well, I think it's a lovely medal,' says Mrs Beatty, but she's made me feel a bit stupid. I have been put on national television and so far it mostly seems to have got me made fun of.

So the day goes the way the days normally go, except with a lot more people staring at me in the playground. I also sign three autographs and Joe 2 pretends he's my agent and says I can pay him back with fifteen per cent of my lunch.

But people seem to forget all about it pretty quickly. I suppose this is a valuable lesson about showbiz.

We play football at break. As usual, I'm not picked first or last, just somewhere in the middle, even though I've been on telly.

Whenever I play football, Mickey stands at the side and watches. Every time I get the ball, she starts whooping and shouting my name and waving at me. It is very off-putting. Once she made a banner with my face on. But it does mean whenever I do a bad kick or let a goal in I can blame it on her for distracting me.

Then we eat our lunch. It's Fish and Chips Friday. There is a vegetarian option that I quite fancy, but, like Dad always says, there's no sense in standing out. Darren Harper will just pounce on me for it.

In maths, we do a test, and I get sixty-five per cent as usual, which Mrs Beatty says is 'alarmingly adequate'.

Joe 2 nudges me and says, 'That's perfect for you – alarmingly adequate is so on-brand!' which I think he heard someone say on TV.

Before I know it, school is over and, for a day that started off so excitingly, it feels like just another average one again.

But at least it's a Friday, so when I get home I don't have to do any homework, and we can do what we always do because Friday night is takeaway night.

Everyone on our street has a curry on a Friday. We normally all go for the korma because that one isn't too spicy. It's a safe, popular choice. But tonight something weird has happened.

When Stan turns up, he says, 'So that's three chicken

kormas . . .' and then pauses. Stan's the man who does the deliveries from the Taj. Now he's just holding out his bag and staring at his piece of paper. 'Er – and one extra-hot garlic chicken jalfrezi with extra chillies?'

He makes a confused face, like he's done something wrong.

'Say that again, Stan?' says Mum.

'One extra-hot garlic chicken jalfrezi with extra chillies?'

Stan looks surprised. Mum looks surprised. Mickey and I make surprised faces at each other. Stan says he's

checked the order three times, but it's definitely right, like someone explaining they'd just seen an alien in the corner shop.

Dad always orders the curries, but tonight there must have been some kind of mix-up. He has never ordered extra-hot garlic chicken jalfrezi with extra chillies before in his life. He orders a korma like everyone else on the street.

'I just . . . fancied a change,' says Dad, looking a bit shy.

None of us knows what to say. A change? On takeaway night?

So we all just walk to the table and watch Dad as he sits down and opens his tinfoil box. We gather round to stare at it.

'It's bright red!' says Mickey. 'It's got green things in it!'

'That's *very* descriptive, Mickey,' says Mum. 'Well done.'

It's not *that* descriptive; she's just said some colours!

Dad picks up his fork and sniffs his steaming takeaway. His eyes immediately start watering and I think his hand is trembling.

'Do you want some of my korma?' asks Mum slowly, looking a bit alarmed.

'No!' says Dad. 'I have ordered the extra-hot garlic chicken jalfrezi with extra chillies because I *wanted* an extra-hot garlic chicken jalfrezi with extra chillies.'

This is extremely unusual behaviour from Dad, but it is the most exciting thing to have happened on a Friday night since that crow flew through our window and Mum had to chase it out with a pepper mill.

Dad slowly takes a bite of his curry and everything seems okay for a minute.

'So how was your day, Joe?' asks Mum, trying to distract everybody, but still glancing at Dad and his curry. 'Did everyone like your medal?'

I want to reply, but I'm keeping an eye on Dad too. He has gone very red.

'He wore it all day,' says Mickey. *But of course I did; it's a medal.*

Dad is staring at the wall and breathing very heavily

through his nose. He looks like one of those TV celebrities in a plastic box in the jungle getting spiders tipped all over them. He has put down his fork and clenched his fists as he very slowly chews.

'Darren Harper said my medal was stupid because it wasn't made out of silver,' I say. 'And he called me "Average Joe".'

Dad's eyes flick towards me. His breathing has got heavier. He has a shiny forehead from all the sweat that's suddenly there.

He takes another forkful of curry and stares at it, then shoves it into his mouth.

'Well, Darren Harper is a big idiot,' says Mickey, which is nice, I guess.

'Is everything okay?' asks Mum, putting her hand on Dad's trembling fist. 'Do you want me to call someone?'

'I am eating my very hot curry,' Dad wheezes, with the voice he uses when he's hit his thumb with a hammer, but wants everyone to think he's fine. 'I just fancied a *change*.'

Dad had to drink three pints of semi-skimmed milk and go to bed early. (Mum phoned the Taj for advice.)

'No one's ever ordered one of those before,' the chef told her. 'So we just sort of made it up.'

The chef also said he'd been delighted to do something different because people on our street only ever order the same thing. But, as I pointed out to Mum, why would we do that when the korma exists?

Mum thinks Dad is having a mid-life crisis. She didn't tell me that to my face. I heard her saying it to Dad through my bedroom wall. She says the same thing occurred to her when he bought that exercise bike he uses to hang his dirty washing on. But apparently Dad is just still really annoyed about the TV show. He says how dare they call me not special at all. He says he ordered the extra-hot garlic chicken jalfrezi with extra chillies to show me that there was more to life than korma. But he also says he's never going to do that again.

I go to sleep a bit worried. What if Dad actually thinks I'm not special too, and that's why he's so upset about the TV man saying it?

What if he thinks I'm a chicken korma?

CHAPTER FOUR

On Saturdays we sleep in, but today is different. Dad's already in the kitchen with Mickey when I get up. He's making his cup of tea. After that, he'll have one slice of brown toast with butter, and then he has his 'good boy' toast, which is for treats, and is white toast with jam. He has done this every single day I have been alive. When we went to Spain, he insisted on bringing his own tea bags. Right now he's listening to that show on the radio that everyone listens to, but I notice he hasn't made any toast. He's eating yoghurt with honey in it.

I give Mickey a Look and she just nods, like she thinks this is totally weird too.

Remind me to look up 'mid-life crisis' in the dictionary.

Also, he's not shaved. Dad shaves every day, even on Sundays. That curry has a lot to answer for.

Anyway, I nearly spit out my cereal when I hear my name on the radio.

'*Joe Smith is his name!*' they're saying. '*The country's most average child!*'

'Joe, that's YOU!' shouts Mickey.

'I know it is. Shhh,' I say.

The man and his friends are all chuckling and, even though I'm trying to laugh along with them, Dad isn't. I'm not surprised – who would be happy when they'd only had yoghurt for breakfast?

One of the radio man's friends goes, '*Let's hope that kid's life isn't one big snoozefest!*' and I wonder what she means.

Mickey looks furious. Dad looks at me as if something had happened that I should be sad about. It did sound a bit like they were making fun of me.

'Who's that?' says Mickey, pointing down the hallway to the front door.

Behind the glass, I can see someone moving, and as I get closer there's the noise of a van chugging and doors being opened. People greeting each other.

At first I'm like, *Oh no, the TV people are back.*

But, when I peek out, it's not them at all.

'Mr Smith?' says this man in a yellow top and grey shorts. 'Delivery.'

He's holding a massive bunch of flowers.

'Dad!' I call out. 'Delivery!'

'No,' says the guy. 'You're Mr Joe Smith, right? I saw you on TV. Sign here.'

There must be a mistake. Mum and Dad get deliveries, not me. Plus, who's sending me *flowers*?

But the man is holding out his screen thing at me.

Then the mechanic from number fourteen walks by.

'Ooh, Joe, are those flowers for me?' he says, using excellent street humour. 'You shouldn't have!'

There's a big *woof* of laughter, and it's only when I look up that I notice more men and women in T-shirts and shorts standing outside even more vans, all of them parked behind the first. Van after van after van. From lots of different companies. Right the way down the street.

'Are you all here for me?' I hear myself say, and every single one of them says, 'Yes.'

* *
 *

Well, everybody loves getting presents, right? I mean, I do, and if I'm average then you probably do too, right?

Last birthday, I got one main present. A new bike. It wasn't the one I'd asked for, which was a gold Speedster 2. It was the old version that Dad got second-hand because it was a big month for bills. But a yellow Speedster 1 was fine by me, even though Darren Harper made fun of it once down the park because it's quite chipped.

But right now? I just could not believe how many presents I was getting. It was like ten birthdays rolled into one.

Plus, I don't think I've ever signed my own name so many times in one go. It was a brilliant chance to practise my autograph, one which no doubt other minor celebrities would be very jealous of.

'What are those on your feet?' goes Mum when she walks into the back garden where I've decided to open all my presents.

'New trainers!' I say. Sure, they're massive and bright lime green and not really my taste, but they're free and they're mine! Mum looks at the note that came with them.

Hi, Joe – we heard you had very average size four feet! Please enjoy our brand-new trainers and don't forget to let us know exactly what you think of them using the enclosed questionnaire!

'I will!' I say out loud, and then I open the next package. It's crammed with chocolate bars.

Hopefully, the most average kid will like the most fragrant new pistachio-nut chocolate bars! Please share them with your most average friends and let us know what you think!

'I will!' I say again, because I suppose what they're really asking for is a thank-you note, and that's only polite, isn't it?

'Hmm,' says Dad, looking suspicious as he sips his tea. Why isn't he delighted that his son is getting loads of free presents?

Mum nudges Dad and says, 'Let him enjoy it', which, because it involves fuss, is *not* like her at all.

All the while, Mickey's been sitting on the plastic garden chair in her panda ears and panda pyjamas and panda slippers, pretending she hasn't noticed the massive pile of boxes.

'You're so lucky, Joe,' she says with a pout. 'Is there anything in there for me?'

I know that there isn't, but I sort of pretend to look, to make her feel better.

'Not today,' I say.

It's a shame that all these companies forgot about Mickey. I guess they just got excited about how average I am and wanted to celebrate with me. Mickey's going to just have to accept that she is not as blessed by being quite as average as me.

'You can have a pistachio-nut chocolate bar if you want,' I say, tossing one at her. 'But don't forget to tell me exactly what you think of it after.'

'Wow, THANK YOU, Joe!' she says, beaming. 'Can I help you open the rest of the packages?'

'Naah, it's okay,' I say because I am the most average child, not her, and this is my life now.

So what's in the next box?

A brand-new type of fluffy sock!

A top-of-the-range marble run!

Then the biggest water blaster you've ever seen!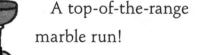

Mickey goes to pick it up, but I ask her not to because I'm not sure that's what the company wants. I feel a bit bad, but I push that aside because there's still more stuff to open.

Mum keeps all the letters that come with them, but they all pretty much say the same thing.

Then there's a new board game called Wham-Blam! – 'The game for people who like saying "Wham-Blam!"' And a huge pile of books, plus some new headphones, a super-cool hoodie with walkie-talkies sewn into the sleeves, a watch that tells me how far I've walked, and a robot dog!

'You've still got that big one to open,' says Mickey a little sulkily, pointing at the package Dad had leaned against the fence.

'Good observation, Mickey!' says Mum. 'You're such a helpful little girl!'

'Do you want me to help, Joe?'

'I'm fine,' I say quickly because she's definitely not

going to open that one. I've been saving it for last.

We all gather round. Even Mum and Dad, who still don't seem as excited about all this as I am. And when I pull the front of the box down . . .

'It's a brand-new bike!' says Mickey. 'But . . . you've already got a bike! Maybe you should give your old one to Joe 2, then you could ride around together.'

'That's really nice of you, Mickey,' says Mum, ruffling her hair, but it's easy to be nice with other people's stuff, isn't it?

And also: this is not *just* a bike.

'Dad! I got a Speedster 3! In GOLD!'

They're not even out yet.

I look at Dad to see how delighted he must be, but he can't have heard me properly.

'This is way better than my old one!' I say, and Dad crosses his arms.

I cannot believe my luck. Being the most average kid in the country might end up making me the luckiest too!

Could today be the day my life peaks? I guess it's a shame if that happens at ten years old, but I'll take it.

'It's the right size!' I say, as Mum hands me the helmet that came with it.

'*Dear Joe, we hope you like this new bike that comes out next year,*' she says, reading the card. '*Please do us a big favour and let us know what you think of it as soon as possible!*'

What do I *think* of it? I LOVE IT!

'I'm going down the park!' I say, strapping my new helmet on.

'Can I come?' asks Mickey.

'Joe! Don't ride the bike through the house!' says Dad.

But I don't have time to answer them because I'm already riding through the living room towards the front door.

CHAPTER FIVE

I knew exactly where Darren Harper would be on a Saturday morning. He'd be down the park. Me and Joe 2 used to meet there until Darren Harper started coming.

Darren Harper's dad is one of those dads who tells his son he is the greatest thing that has ever walked the Earth and that the rest of us are losers and wimps. My dad says it's because Darren Harper's dad is making sure everyone knows Darren is the Chosen One. Darren got an electric guitar for his birthday and when he played it in assembly his dad recorded the whole thing on his phone and emailed it to all the other parents and said Darren was the new Jimi Hendrix (I don't know who that is).

Anyway, that's when the school banned us from bringing our own instruments in. I am not saying Darren is terrible at guitar, I'm just saying a lot of people could have died from music poisoning that day.

But Darren thinks he's brilliant at guitar because Darren is told he's brilliant at *everything*.

'Oh, hi, *Average Joe*,' he sneers when I get near the swing that he's standing on. But then he notices it. 'What's *that*?'

'This?' I say. 'Oh, it's just a Speedster 3 in gold.'

I see a gigantic flash of jealousy on his face.

'Yeah, no big deal,' I say. 'Just one of the perks of being distinctly *average*, I guess.'

Ha. I'm showing him!

'*Lucky*. Where did you get it?' he says. 'Only I'm getting one too, you know.'

'Yeah? Weird, cos they're not out yet. This is the first one.'

He doesn't know what to say.

'Anyway, it was just one of my presents this morning. Like these big green trainers.'

'Why?' he asks. 'Is it your birthday?'

'Nah,' I say, all casual because I am *really* enjoying this. 'I just got all this free stuff because I'm so not special. Because I'm so average.'

He just stares and stares at me. I can tell he wants to say something mean, but he is too confused and annoyed and also I've got a Speedster 3.

Then I went to get Joe 2 and told him we had a lot of chocolate to get through back at mine. Like Mickey said, he doesn't have a bike, so he ran alongside me. I'd told him it was really important we ate all the chocolate as quickly as possible, so that we could give feedback to the chocolate people who were waiting to hear from me. He couldn't stop laughing.

So we sit cross-legged in the garden and line up bar after bar of chocolate, ready for consumption.

'Can I have another weird nutty one?' asks Mickey from the doorway.

'Not right now,' I say. 'We're working and require privacy.'

Though Mickey still hangs about, probably just to annoy me, and Joe 2 says, 'See you in a bit though, Mickey!' and smiles. His teeth are covered in chocolate.

Joe 2 doesn't have any brothers or sisters, which I think must be why he's always so nice to Mickey.

'This is horrible,' says Joe 2, trying not to spit his chocolate out. 'What *is* it?'

'It's pistachio-nut chocolate, dude,' I say, and then I look at the label properly. 'With lavender and hints of rosemary.'

'It's like eating one of those blue blocks they put in toilets!'

I agree, though I wonder how he knows that.

Joe 2 is a trusted friend and someone whose opinions are usually the same as mine. It's why we're such good pals. If it wasn't for me, I'm pretty sure Joe 2 could have been Britain's most average child if he'd tried just a little harder. But Joe 2 gets very slightly better marks than me, and he is ever-so-slightly shorter, so I'm sorry, Joe 2, but you can't be me.

'What shall I put?' I say, holding up the questionnaire they'd placed in the box.

Joe 2 says, 'If they want you to be honest, I'd say, "Lavender has no place in a chocolate bar and you should probably work on your choice of nut."'

I wrote exactly that on the questionnaire and then we did the same for Wham-Blam!

Feedback: It is not quite enough fun to have a game where all you do is say, 'Wham-Blam!'

Then the fluffy socks. Joe 2 tried one on and I tried the other.

Feedback: Absolutely perfect – no improvements necessary. Well done.

It is quite nice giving my opinion on things. Normally my opinion goes largely unheard. Sometimes on TV you see those grown-ups who say really horrible things about other people. They make fun of them for being poor, or a bit unfit, or for really random stuff like where they were born, as if that's something anyone can help. They get really famous for saying these horrible things, and everyone listens to what they say. Or you get those people who say really amazing things about world peace and recycling, and everyone listens to them as well and puts them on magazine covers, but forgets to do what they say.

It is about time the people in between got heard, which is why I think it's really important to make sure I finish all these disgusting chocolate bars.

Just then I hear my mum go, 'Joe . . . ?' and I realise we are basically sitting on a pile of chocolate wrappers.

'Yes?' I say, hoping we don't smell too much of lavender or blue toilet blocks.

The man in our living room didn't know whether I'd won the competition or whether Joe 2 had.

I set him straight immediately, of course.

'It's not him,' I said, pointing at Joe 2 and trying not to notice that he looked a bit hurt. 'It's me. I am the country's most average child.'

Then the man said this was a private matter so I had to send Joe 2 home because time is money.

'I could wait outside?' says Joe 2, and I don't think that's a bad idea, but the man shakes his head.

'Joe 2,' I say, 'your work today is done. Leave us.'

It's not that I don't want to share, it's just that my luck has really changed and I've got free chocolate and own two bikes and I really need to make the most of it.

Mum and Dad sit on the sofa next to Mickey, and the man is in the big armchair. Mum swaps an awkward look with Dad. Then the man starts to concentrate on me so much that it feels like it's just me and him in the room, which is creepy.

He tells me his name is Mr Albert. He is wearing a navy blue suit and has hair the colour of gravel. He tells me that he's travelled a long way to come to Didcot today. He tells me he has a very important job that helps make the world a better place, and isn't making the world a better place what we're all here for?

I'm listening to his words and he's really convincing, and all I keep doing is nodding.

But Mr Albert has this low voice that you have to lean in to hear and he has this way of talking that makes some words feel like they're almost dancing in the air, the way magicians talk when they're doing a trick.

I feel a bit dizzy from having to concentrate on what this strange grown-up is saying, and I have to keep checking Mum and Dad are there as Mr Albert tells me I would not only be helping my town, but I would be helping make children happier all over the whole country – maybe even the world.

'Don't you think children deserve to be happy?' he goes on, in his weird, low voice, and I go, 'Yeah.'

And he goes, 'We all think children deserve to be happy, don't we?' and I go, 'Yeah,' and it's amazing how much he says that I agree with.

And he tells me he's so pleased we're 'on the same page' and how he was sure that I wouldn't be 'another Mediocre Mary'.

And, when he's finished, he stands up and smooths down his tie and buttons his suit jacket and says, 'Nice to have you on board, Joe Smith.'

MR ALBERT

CHAPTER SIX

Mum seemed quite relieved when Mr Albert had gone.

She goes a little quiet around people who make speeches because people who make speeches always seem to think they know what they're on about. Dad says they're just people who make speeches. He says it's the quiet people who tend to actually think about what to say. That makes Mum feel better.

Anyway, when Mr Albert's gone, my mum and dad

start speaking all low and send Mickey off to stare at the tablet, and I sit there, not quite knowing what's going on.

I *was* listening to Mr Albert, but I was mostly hearing *how* he spoke rather than what he said. And I was thinking about how it made me feel, rather than what it meant.

'I'm going to say no,' I hear Dad say.

'No to what?' I say.

'Wait,' says Mum, and she takes Dad into the kitchen.

I press my ear up against the wall and I can hear them.

'Are you going to do it?' says Mickey, sitting on the stairs with Mum's iPad, playing *Panda-monium*.

'Do what?'

'Do what the weird man said?' she says.

It's incredibly annoying that she seems to know what

he said and I don't. Obviously, I'm not going to ask her to tell me.

Then I hear Mum raise her voice ever so slightly.

'So now you're worried that we've brought him up to be average and told him to just blend in! Well, this could be two birds with one stone – this changes all that. This makes him special!'

'Well, if he's special, he's not average, is he? And if he's not average then, according to these people, he's not special!' says Dad. 'Plus, it will be a lot of fuss.'

'I do worry sometimes that I don't take enough chances,' says Mum, after a pause. 'Like the van.'

'Something about it is odd,' says Dad. 'Won't letting Joe do it mean he'll grow up thinking that we think he's . . . average?'

'Not necessarily,' says Mum. 'And, like you always used to say, there's nothing wrong with being average, as if that even exists anyway.'

'We're *not* average!' says Dad. 'I was in a band!'

You know how I told you Dad always reminds us he was in that band? I think he actually does it to remind himself.

'The thing we're not saying,' says Mum, 'is that the money would come in handy.'

So I creep back to Mickey and ask her what exactly it was Mr Albert said as I'd been a bit overwhelmed at the time.

And she said it was his company that sponsored the search for the most average child in the country. She said Mr Albert's company liked to know what people were thinking because then they'd know what people liked. And, if they knew what most people liked, then they'd be able to make *more* of it for *everyone*. She said his company did things like this in lots of different countries. And they were already planning some very exciting changes right here in Didcot for starters, and if they went well they'd make the same changes in lots of other towns and cities too.

To me this sounded brilliant. Imagine if every kid got the one thing for their birthday that they were guaranteed to like? Imagine if every film you watched, according to the research, you were guaranteed to like? If everything was the right thing, nothing would be rubbish!

(Also, if Mum and Dad let me do it, it means I'll get loads more presents.)

So, when they come out of the kitchen, looking all worried, I say, 'Mum and Dad, I really want to help Mr Albert to help the families of this world by giving them what they want, especially if it means I get more presents, etc.'

But no one has time to respond because Darren Harper's dad's at the door.

Darren Harper's dad owns the Mazda dealership and he gets to drive as many different brand-new Mazdas as he wants.

'Mr Smith,' he goes, sounding a bit sarcastic and leaning his hand on our door frame like he owns the place.

'Mr Harper,' says Dad.

My dad and Mr Harper have history. It all started when Dad asked Mr Harper to calm down at a school football match. Mr Harper kept shouting really loudly at Darren, which was a bit scary and embarrassing. He kept yelling at him to score more, but that's easier said than done, isn't it? He seemed to think Darren was letting him down on purpose and making him look bad, and, even though Mum begged Dad not to, Dad wandered over and told Mr Harper to shoosh his lips up. Now they look like cowboys, trying to work out if the other one was going to shoot first.

'So I haven't seen you at badminton lately,' goes Darren's dad, like it's a crime.

'I've given up,' says Dad. 'My knees are spent.'

'Spent?' Darren's dad laughs. 'They're halfway through their overdraft!'

I don't know what any of this means, but they sound like jokes that aren't jokes.

'Anyway, question for you,' says Darren's dad, squinting like he's cool.

I can see Darren sitting in the Mazda outside, the window slowly fogging up, staring at me like he's annoyed.

'We're just planning our holiday –' his dad smiles – 'and wondered where you were going for yours?'

'We haven't thought about it yet,' says my dad, but I know that's not true because Mum and Dad told us we couldn't really afford one this year.

'Good to know,' says Darren Harper's dad, turning away and starting to walk down the path.

'Is it?' goes Dad.

Darren Harper's dad shrugs. 'Just wanted to know

where the *average* person was going this year,' he says, 'so we can do something *better*.'

Darren Harper has definitely told his dad about my new bike. And obviously Darren Harper's dad is annoyed because he couldn't get a Speedster 3 for Darren. So it's a victory for the Smiths! But Dad seems really bothered.

'And so it begins,' he says with a sigh, sitting down on the sofa, scratching his stubble. 'People are going to be coming up to me all the time and asking me questions like, "What should the average person have for their tea tonight?" or, "How many pairs of underpants does the average person get through a year?" I'm just going to be Mr Average of Didcot, but I was *in a band*! I had a *guitar*! A bright red *Fender American Stratocaster*!'

I don't know why Dad isn't more flattered by all this. Maybe someone will send him a Speedster and then he won't be so grumpy.

He sighs again and scratches his face.

'Should I have a shave, Joe? What do you think?'

Why's he asking me this? Because the average child has no opinion either way.

'I looked it up and one shave takes, on average, ten minutes,' he says. 'If you add all that up, an average man spends an average of one hundred and fifty days of his average life shaving.' He rubs his eyes like he's in pain. 'Imagine how many gigs I could have played with Samurai! in those one hundred and fifty days.'

Just then Mum's phone dings and she jumps.

'It's a text from Mr Albert,' she says. 'So have we decided? Should we do it?'

'Do what?' I ask.

'Joe, just say if you don't want to,' she says. 'It's your decision whether you help with the research or not.'

The research? Is that what they're calling it? That sounds brilliant! I start nodding furiously.

Dad puts his head in his hands, then looks up with a face like he's really thinking about something. Darren Harper's dad must have really put him on edge.

'Tell him yes,' says Dad.

CHAPTER SEVEN

I have to bring a responsible adult with me, but I didn't have one of them right now so I brought Dad.

Dad kept telling me to play things cool and just act normal and to remember that these people weren't my friends, but when I found out what the first stop was I couldn't help but be excited. It was Sunday and we were going to the head office of the company that owned some of the best restaurants in the country.

They owned Fasta Pasta and, best of all, Burger Joint, which I'd never tell Nico I love because he always calls those places 'soulless' and goes off on a big rant about it. As if a restaurant needs a soul!

Anyway, we were off to the HQ where they came up with all their ground-breaking ideas, like putting an extra slice of bacon on a cheeseburger and calling it 'the Ultimate Burger'. I mean, how do you even come up with that?!

Dad stopped the car and we saw a big sign outside their normal-looking brick building that said WELCOME, JOE! and there was a red carpet from the car park, past the bins, to the automatic double doors. It was absolutely magical.

Mr Albert said there'd be some people ready to meet us, but that we had to be done by 2 p.m. and he'd be arranging transport for us straight after. I thought that was a bit weird because we had Dad's car, but then all the top bosses walked through the doors and started applauding me.

'You must be Average Dad!' says one of them to Dad, but then they all stop looking at him and look at me, like I'm a precious jewel or something, which I suppose I sort of am now.

'Thank you so much for coming, Joe,' says one of them. I can't remember which because, apart from some of them wearing dresses and some of them wearing suits, 'business grown-ups' all look the same.

I don't know why Dad said these people weren't my friends. Maybe it's because Dad doesn't really have many friends himself. He had the band a long, long time ago in the dark ages, but since then it was always just people from work. Plus, this lot were being super friendly, and before I know it I'm in this big long room. And there's this big long table that seems to stretch off into the distance. There's plate after plate of food, all looking exactly like they do in the photos you get in takeaways. Have you ever looked at your actual meal after looking at one of those photos? It usually looks like someone's sat on it. But these ones were perfect.

There's a plate with, like, the world's most awesome cheeseburger on it.

There's a plate with a chicken burger and a double crispy bacon triple-decker on it.

There's hot dogs and fried chicken and a pizza called 'the Supremo' because it's got some extra bacon on it.

There's cheesy fries and normal fries and curly fries and 'Super-size Prize Fries', which are big fries with some, well, bacon on them.

There's chocolate milkshakes, strawberry milkshakes, banana milkshakes.

It just goes on and on, like there's going to be about a hundred people coming in for their lunch at any moment.

'Is this your staff canteen?' I go, feeling my mouth water. And this is where the main business grown-

up leans down and puts a hand on my shoulder and whispers, 'This is our top-secret testing lab. And you're our new tester.'

And I realise all this food is for me.

ALL THIS FOOD IS FOR ME!

'Dad, am I allowed?' I say because this is too good to be true.

Dad says it's up to me.

So I slowly pick up a cheeseburger, like this is a trick and I'm going to get caught.

And, as I do, all the grown-ups reach into their pockets and get notepads out.

'He went for the cheeseburger first!' whispers a woman. 'The cheeseburger should be our main cut-through item for Q3 starting at midnight.'

 I don't know what that means, but they're all still staring at me. So I take a big bite out of the cheeseburger

and it is like heaven, unless you're a vegetarian, of course, or have issues with cheese.

Sweet, warm ketchup squelches to the sides of my mouth and I chew very deliberately, like I'm really concentrating, in case they try to grab it off me.

'It's GOOD!' I say, and I'm surprised because everybody cheers and whoops and high-fives 'I really like the onion.'

'He likes the onion!' shouts a man.

'But I feel like maybe there's a bit too much ketchup?'

'You IDIOT, Gary!' shouts the first woman, hitting some guy on the arm, and it is then that I realise my power.

'Promise me you'll open a Burger Joint in Didcot!' I say, a bit giddy, because we don't have a Burger Joint in Didcot, let alone a Pizza Palace or a Fasta Pasta.

'Would the average child like a Burger Joint in Didcot?' asks a man, making notes. 'Because we can move in hours.'

'Are you kidding?' I say, and everyone laughs. I'm obviously delightful!

Next it's the hot dog and everyone shuffles behind me as I reach over for it and take a bite.

'Juicy!' I say. 'Magical!'

There's a big sigh of relief from behind me, and then I go for the popcorn chicken bucket and a chicken burger.

'Tender,' I say. 'Though a *little* overspiced!'

Everyone makes interested noises and writes down 'a little overspiced' and I am really getting into this.

Everything I say is suddenly very important and meaningful. I could say anything. I could say, 'Yes, this Diet Coke is nice, but I'm afraid it's a little runny,' and

everyone would write down 'The Coke is too runny!' and then talk for ages about how to make it more solid.

Dad told me that companies sometimes spend thousands of pounds getting loads and loads of people to sit together in little groups for ages and discuss things. Then someone has to write all these opinions down and work out what it all means and it sounds incredibly boring. Why not just make good stuff that people like? Anyway, Dad told me on the way here that, instead of all that, these people are just going to ask *me* what I think and then put that into a computer. Because, if I'm the average kid, then whatever I like is what most other kids will like too!

'Is *this* better, Joe?' asks a woman who's just run out of another room. She's short of breath and carrying a chicken burger. She holds it up to my mouth. 'We de-spiced it!'

'Far superior,' I say, after a nibble. 'You did it!'

I saw in a film once someone said that power ruins people. But now I don't think it's true that power ruins people because I suddenly have loads of it and I'm using it to make chicken burgers taste nicer.

A little while later, I have also improved their cheeseburgers, hamburgers, hot dogs, pizzas, falafels and tacos HUGELY. You really do owe me your thanks.

I've been having a great time, but Dad's just been sitting on a small plastic chair in the corner with a sad cardboard box of chicken nuggets, chewing and staring at a wall.

And then one of the business grown-ups goes, 'Okay! Let's make our way to the *dessert* hangar!'

CHAPTER EIGHT

I always thought you could never have enough ice cream, but now I definitely know that you can absolutely have enough ice cream.

I am stuffed. I probably don't even have any blood in me any more, just strawberry sauce. I reckon if a scientist did my DNA test they'd think I was eighty per cent vanilla. If you popped a cherry on my head, people would think they could lick me. I might see if

Mum will let me swap my bed for a cone.

And, when the car Mr Albert has arranged comes to pick us up, it is not what I expected *at all*.

It's a Ferrari.

Now me, Dad and a guy with a clipboard on his lap are all crushed up together, trying to pretend it's normal to be in a Ferrari. Dad's in the back on the fold-down seats. His head is touching the ceiling so he has to bend his neck. I wouldn't call a Ferrari a very practical family car. You never see a Ferrari with a baby seat. I guess that's also because not many babies drive Ferraris.

That was a joke, sorry. I'm just in a really good mood remembering all this.

'What do you think of this car, Joe?' says the clipboard man, before we set off. 'What do you think of the colour?'

'It's very yellow,' I say.

'Very yellow,' says the man, even though I'm right next to him, and he ticks a box that says 'Likes Yellow'.

It's nice he wants my opinion on the car. I don't know

how many children buy Ferraris. He starts the car and it roars to life.

'And, Average Dad?' he asks Dad. 'What do you think?'

'My name is not Average Dad,' snaps Dad. 'And I am quite happy with our very practical family car, thank you very much.'

Oh my gosh, Darren Harper would be so jealous if he saw me in this.

'Put down "this car is much better than a Mazda", will you?' I say. 'So, um, where are we going?'

I don't really mind where we're going, to be fair, but I hope we get there quite quickly because I am totally full of various different milkshakes.

'What do you think would make your mum or dad buy one of these cars?' says the man, ignoring my question. 'Do you like the leather steering wheel?'

'Oh, you can't beat a leather steering wheel,' I say, even though I haven't the faintest idea about steering wheels and almost never talk to my friends about them. 'But I think if you added maybe seven seats and a much bigger boot and maybe an ejector seat for when Mum says we've had too many snacks that might help?'

He writes all this down, but he still hasn't answered my question about where we're going. We seem to be heading to the motorway. People we overtake wave at the car and take pictures of us on their phones, assuming quite correctly there is a celebrity inside.

'Would you like some chewing gum?' says the man, suddenly pulling out six different packs and fanning them out like they're playing cards, or actually just like they're a fan.

I take one and he says, 'Spearmint,' to himself, as if that's really important.

'Could I have one?' asks Dad, but the man says no because they're only meant for me.

Poor Dad. I decide that I will give him mine when I've finished chewing it.

That must have put Dad in a bad mood because, as we pass a sign saying Milton Keynes is thirty miles away, Dad taps the clipboard man on the shoulder and says, 'Where *exactly* are we off to?'

CHAPTER NINE

When we get to Milton Keynes, I am delighted!

Milton Keynes is the best. When you get a birthday party invite and it says Milton Keynes on it, you know you're in for a treat. Milton Keynes has all the best places to eat in the world, and if I hadn't already just eaten everything in the world I would probably have another cheeseburger.

Loads of people from Didcot move to Milton Keynes,

because, even though once it was just a big field, now it is perfection. Some prime minister, thousands of years ago, decided to build a 'new town' there, and they were able to take everything they had learned about humans since the dawn of time and make sure Milton Keynes had it all: shoe shops, launderettes, a dry ski slope, an indoor skydiving centre – everything humankind could ever need in one place. Personally, I would have put a dome on top to keep it dry. Now that people are listening to my thoughts at last, this is something I might raise with the Queen.

I bet, even though she's got castles and whatnot, the Queen herself would agree that building the Hollywood Bowl bowling centre in Milton Keynes is probably the gold standard of human achievement.

Anyway, my eyes must be as big as Hollywood Bowl bowling balls as we pass it because the clipboard man says, 'Oh, Joe, it gets even better than that.'

'Mr Smith, this is how it's going to work,' says a lady with grey hair called Mrs Larson.

She's a bit strict, but very respectful, which as a VIP I appreciate. She is pacing round the Ferrari and I am keeping up with her, like we are just two totally normal business people discussing our important business around a yellow sports car. I wonder if she lives in Milton Keynes. I don't know how you could get to sleep at night if you lived in Milton Keynes. Imagine being that close to so many water slides.

But I'm finding it quite hard to keep a lid on my excitement because we are outside another big brown building on an industrial estate, and this one is called Toy Warehouse International.

'You, Mr Smith,' she says, adjusting her glasses, 'are going to enter Toy Warehouse International through the front entrance.' And she points at it.

'Front entrance,' I repeat. Like I was going to try to get in through the toilet window.

'You will then have five minutes,' she says.

'Good,' I say. But I don't really understand and I give Dad a Look.

'Five minutes for what exactly?' asks Dad, helping me out, because I don't want to look stupid and would prefer it if it was Dad that looked stupid.

'There are fourteen million toys in that warehouse,' she says, ignoring him, 'and do you know which one of them is the best?'

'No,' I say.

'Do you know which of them will appeal most to the average child?'

'No.'

'Do you know which of them every child will want to find under the Christmas tree this year?'

'No!' I say.

'Neither do we,' she says. 'But maybe if you run in there, and grab whatever your heart desires in five minutes or less, we'll begin to find out.'

Dad looks at me, shocked, and I look at him, even more shocked.

'They want to watch you while you grab the toys you want the most,' he says, 'so they can see what they have the best chance of making every parent in the country buy.'

'Wow!' I say because has anyone ever said a BETTER or HAPPIER sentence than that? 'You're saying I have five minutes to grab whatever I want?'

'Whatever you can fit in your trolley,' says Mrs Larson.

I could cry just at the thought of it.

'And it's mine to keep?'

'Yours to keep.'

I make her wait a second before I say it.

'Mrs Larson, I would be willing to do this for my country.'

'Good,' says Mrs Larson. 'No Mediocre Marys here.'

That's the second time I've heard these people say 'Mediocre Mary'. I suppose it must be a bit like 'Average Joe' but more equal and appropriate for the modern age.

I'll ask Dad later, but first I have to calm my breathing and slow down my heart rate because Mrs Larson is about to press the stopwatch to start my five minutes.

And then she holds that stopwatch in the air, and it goes . . . *BLEEP*.

 I run straight towards the double doors and push them wide open so that they slam against the walls. Several people with clipboards run in behind me.

'Oh my gosh,' I say because I am in a brightly lit warehouse, with ride-on cars and basketballs and bouncy castles and a giant stuffed panda and games consoles and literally everything I have ever seen on TV and gone, 'Can I please have that for Christmas?' – which is most things I see on TV.

This is my dream come true!

I take a trolley and start to run down the first aisle and grab something.

'Pinball Wizard!' shouts a man behind me. 'He chose a Pinball Wizard!'

'Alert the factory!' yells another.

Then I grab a baseball set, and a Stomp Rocket, but then I pause in the grabbing because I've got a lot of aisles to get through yet!

I push past the footballs and the board games and the giant panda, grab a radio-controlled plane and turn the corner.

This is the educational aisle. It's all wooden puzzles and globes.

Haha. I'm not falling for *that*!

I spin the trolley round and find the next aisle. This is more like it!

'He's got a games controller and headset!' yells a man.

'Den kit!' yells another.

'Laser guns!'

'Mega Lego City set!'

And then Mrs Larson yells, 'Two minutes remaining!'

We get home around teatime and the Ferrari man unloads all my new toys from the trailer he had to attach to the back. It is nice to have people to do things for me. I suppose in many ways I have become like a prince or something.

'Bring me anything nice, Joe?' asks the mechanic from number fourteen as he watches the stuff being brought in.

'Haha, good street humour!' I laugh. 'But no.'

Dad's being a bit quiet. He's probably just overwhelmed. It's been a big day for him and all he's eaten were those chicken nuggets. Plus, he wasn't allowed to ride home in the Ferrari because he had to drive his boring old car.

'Well?' Mum is in the hallway, with Mickey standing

next to her. 'Tell me all about it! Was it all right? Did they work you too hard?'

'I had hot dogs and cheeseburgers and fries and milkshakes and pizzas and ice cream and a big banana covered in chocolate!' I say. 'And Dad had some nuggets.'

Mickey smiles and says, 'Wow!' but then adds, 'We had meaty pasta and Mum let me do the chilli blobs,' and I say, 'That's nice', just to be nice.

'And then we got in that Ferrari that's just parked outside,' I say, and as I turn round I see Darren Harper cycling slowly past my house, trying to pretend he couldn't see it, but looking well jealous. He never cycles past our house. I know exactly why he's here. It's because me being special is driving him crazy.

'And then we went to a giant toy warehouse and I was allowed to choose ANYTHING,' I say very loudly, hoping he hears me as he quickly cycles off.

'You could choose anything?' says Mickey, and she looks excited.

Mickey gazes longingly at all the boxes as they come into the house. She spots the Lego and laser guns as they go past.

'Was there any panda stuff there?' she asks.

'Panda stuff?' I say. 'Er, no. There were no panda things.'

I mean, there was that *one* panda thing. The big stuffed panda. But I don't need to tell Mickey that. And, anyway, this was about what the average kid wants. Not the average kid's sister.

'It's good you had a good time,' says Mickey. 'You're so lucky.' And it's nice that she's pleased for me, but I actually feel a bit bad.

Mickey seems in a weird quiet mood, so Mum tries to make her feel better by arranging her tea in the shape of a panda. Because I'm a good brother, I do not point out that pandas have black eyes, not green ones made out of peas. It takes everything I have not to do that.

Dad hasn't said much since we got back, but now that Mum's seen I had a good time she's excited for me.

'Do you have any idea what you're doing tomorrow?' she says. 'Mr Albert hasn't texted the details yet.'

'Can *I* come tomorrow?' asks Mickey.

'It's Monday – you've got school,' I say.

'How come *you* don't have school?' she says, and Mum and Dad swap a guilty look.

I don't know why they'd feel guilty about this. All that happened was that Mr Chesil first said I couldn't have this week off because it was illegal and he'd go to prison, but then changed his mind when Mr Albert's company offered the school some new computers. They said it might help with the Ofsted results. So Mr Chesil said that actually he didn't mind turning a blind eye, seeing as he now understood my research was so important to the happiness of the world's children.

I hope Mr Chesil understands that I am like Malala or Greta Thunberg, in that it is my sacrifice of a week at school that may change the world for the better. I would not be surprised if he names the new IT room the 'Joe Smith Room for Childhood Excellence' and, in fact, I will definitely suggest it.

'So we should talk about our holiday this year!' says Mum, looking excited. Mum likes to have something to look forward to. She says, even if things haven't worked out in the past, there's always the future.

I imagine they'll just decide on Spain again. The only place I've ever really wanted to go to is Space Mountain in Florida. You get to do all this space stuff and ride massive space roller coasters and pretend you're an astronaut. *That's* a holiday.

'I thought we couldn't afford a holiday?' says Mickey.

'Is Mr Albert paying for that too?'

The way she says that makes it sound like Mr Albert is doing something wrong in giving the school computers or giving Mum and Dad money in return for child labour.

'Where do you think we should go, Joe?' says Dad. 'Where is the best place we could go to have exactly the right amount of fun? Not too much, not too little. Nothing surprising or different. Just *very* average.'

'Hey,' says Mum, like Dad is being weird, but I think it's a very good question.

'I mean, we *could* do something different,' he says. 'We could go cheese rolling in Devon, if that appealed?'

Cheese rolling? (I looked it up later that night. It's where people literally roll cheese down a hill. The things people did before the internet!)

'Or we could go bog-snorkelling in Ireland,' he says.

(Again, I had to look this up. It's where you put a snorkel on and swim through a bog. That's it. That's the whole thing. I mean, why would you swim through a bog when you could go to the leisure centre or somewhere with water slides?)

'Or we could go to Norway for the annual wife-carrying competition.'

(I kid you not. There is a village in Norway where all the men see who can carry their wives through an obstacle course the fastest. I mean, hello? I'm not even married. Is Dad suggesting I get married just so I can carry someone over a wall someone has stuck in a field? Because that is no reason to sacrifice my freedom at such a young age. Also: sexist. What if *I* want to be carried instead?)

Dad has clearly gone mad. Maybe his nuggets were poisoned.

'But no,' he continues, as we sit there, silently listening to this oddness, 'those are not things *we* would do because *we* are a *normal* family who work all day in offices and *don't* play in bands called Samurai!'

He puts his fork down, stands up and leaves the table.

'Mum, what's wrong with Dad?' asks Mickey.

But I think I might know. I think he's just jealous of me.

'Dad,' I say at bedtime, trying to make things a bit better. 'If this is about the chicken nuggets, I'll make sure I share the burgers with you next time.'

He smiles as he sits on my bed.

'It's not that, Joe,' he says, ruffling my hair. 'I want you to have all the burgers in the world. But I've realised I want them to be great burgers. Not just average burgers.'

He strokes my cheek.

'When you or Mickey have a hamburger, Joe, I want it to be the exact right hamburger for you. The hamburger that makes you happy. Not some hamburger that's been designed to be sold at the exact right price and in the exact right box because someone has decided that

hamburger will appeal to you and everyone else, but a unique hamburger that speaks to your very soul.'

I feel like he's saying 'hamburger' too much.

'You deserve a hamburger that's different from anyone else's. Don't just take the burger that people tell you that you should want. Maybe I haven't told you this enough, but it's okay for your burger to be different. It will set you apart because you will be doing something brave. And you will make great friends that you should hang on to because you're part of a very special band.'

Band?

'I mean burger.'

I think Dad might be drunk.

But maybe I do get what he's saying. Maybe he's saying I should have a nice burger.

I didn't actually work it out for a while yet. He wasn't really talking about burgers at all.

Then Mum pops her head round the door and yells, 'I'm washing your swimming trunks!'

CHAPTER TEN

There were a few things that happened before I could use my swimming trunks.

First off, at 8 a.m. on the dot, a video-games truck pulled up outside our house.

Yes. A video-games truck. I mean, come on! And a guy jumped out and told me I had to spend the next two hours playing whatever video games I wanted! But that I had to do it seriously – playing games wasn't just about fun.

This was the best start to a Monday morning you could ever imagine.

He had everything in the back of his massive truck, he said. Huge plasma screens, cool gaming chairs, headsets you could talk into, and loads of games that weren't even out yet!

'See you later, Joe,' says Mickey a bit sulkily, as Dad clicks her seat belt in. She has fought going to school today as hard as she can. She says she's fed up of me having all the fun. I mean, talk about unfair! It's not my fault I'm special!

'See you later, Mickey,' I say.

'Have fun today,' she says quietly. 'Maybe after school we could play a game together?'

Then I spot Joe 2 waving out of his car on the way to school, and his mum stops right outside our house.

'Mum, can I get out and see the truck?' says Joe 2, all giddy.

'Well, just for a minute or so, if it's okay with Joe?' she replies, smiling.

I think about it for a mo. I mean, Joe 2 would love this. And it'd only be one quick go before school. But I look at my new watch and remember Mr Albert telling Joe 2 to leave.

'Actually, I've got to crack on,' I say. 'I only have this for two hours and then I've got to test out all the water slides at the brand-new Ultra Aqua World.'

'Oh,' says Joe 2.

'But have a good day at school, dude!' I say generously. It is nice to be nice.

Darren Harper cycles past. He's always cycling past

at the moment, isn't he? He sees the truck and his face darkens.

'You don't deserve any of this,' he says.

'Behold – ULTRA AQUA WORLD!' says a man with a beard named Simon.

Sorry, I mean the man is named Simon. I don't mean the man has a beard named Simon.

Anyway, Simon's top is too small for him and he's wearing swimming trunks that look like little pants. I really think he should have made more of an effort for my arrival. He presses a button that makes a big blue curtain drop to the floor, and everyone around us applauds as we see what's behind it.

A massive, endless, perfectly still tropical swimming pool with colourful slides, waterfalls, splash pads and giant inflatables.

I do not applaud, or show any excitement, as I want to remain professional. The video-games guy made me realise that this is my job now. They don't want some over excited kid. They want an expert. Because, if I take it seriously, then I'm earning it, and then I *do* deserve it, don't I?

I *do* deserve it, Darren Harper.

I think Dad is surprised by my newfound maturity because he just looks at me, puzzled that I didn't react more.

'Maybe we shouldn't tell Mickey you had too much fun today,' he says carefully.

No problem because, remember, I have to act like this isn't just fun. It is my duty.

So that I can remember what these slides look like, I take my brand-new phone out of my pocket and snap a quick picture. Right after the games truck left, the phone van had arrived. A lady in dungarees had jumped out and told me to pick any phone I wanted and just let them know what I thought of it.

The phone was mine to keep, but, I mean, of course it

was. Everything is free at the moment. I chose a myPhone 15. Joe 2's dad has got the *old* version of this. I can't wait to tell Joe 2 I've got a better phone than his dad! He will be delighted for me.

'So what do you think of the slides?' asks Simon, like a puppy looking for a pat on the head. I can tell he wants me to say they're brilliant, which is a bit annoying.

The Ultra Aqua World people have obviously put a lot of money into this. I know that for a fact because Dad once tried to build us a water slide in the back garden and he used all his B&Q club points, but then we couldn't get on it because Mum called it a death trap. Mind you, Mum calls a lot of things death traps.

Anyway, there's that hot chlorine feel and smell that gets you all excited in this place. Usually, there'd be loads of splashing sounds and screaming and laughing, but today it is very grown-up and quiet. There were more water slides than I had ever seen in one place. Red ones, blue ones, twisty ones, bumpy ones, and one that went right outside the building before coming back in again.

'Would you like the wave machine on?' says Simon.

'Not at first, Simon,' I say seriously. 'Allow me to experience these water slides in their purest form before we add any extra elements. I must judge them on their own merits.'

Do you know what happens then? Simon actually *bows*.

I've heard that expression, 'I bow to your knowledge.' That's exactly what Simon just did. It is becoming clear to the grown-ups that I am not just some kid. I am to be treated with enormous respect.

I look at Dad, hoping he's impressed, but he's just staring at me, confused.

The best slide, incidentally, turned out to be the Swirler. They told me they had worked really hard on it, but I told them it needed one more swirly bit at the end, and they all nodded, a bit annoyed. I mean, I know nothing about designing slides, and I bet adding another swirly bit will

take ages and cost loads, but you've got to say *something*, haven't you?

What I should have asked them to add was more kids.

I mean, I had fun, but it isn't quite the same when it's just you on your own. There's no one to laugh with. Some things are supposed to be shared.

I've never been to a water park without my whole family before. Dad hasn't even got his trunks on this time.

I might even have liked it more if Mickey had been there, I realised with amazement.

Mickey would have loved it.

Don't tell her, but I actually really, really wish Mickey had been there.

CHAPTER ELEVEN

When we got home, Mum was back from work and was really annoyed because as soon as she got back some of the other mums had started coming round to ask her loads of questions.

Some of the local dads had started doing it with Dad too, just like he said they would.

The other parents seem to think that, because my parents are now known nationally as extremely average people, they will be able to solve any problems they have in their private lives.

Mum is complaining because there is the internet for that, but people have seen a local opportunity.

'Is it normal that my husband dries his socks in the microwave?' one of them had asked Mum as soon as she got to the door. 'Would the average husband do that?'

'Well . . . no?' Mum had replied, just trying to say the right thing.

'*Thank* you,' the lady had said, looking grim. 'I'm going straight home to tell Martin!'

Another mum had wanted to know how long the 'average man' took to load the dishwasher because hers took absolutely *aaaages* and it was really winding her up.

Also, one of the older dads with white hair had cornered Dad when he got out of his car and said, 'Is it normal that when my wife snores she does it so loudly that all the photos fall off the wall? How loudly does *your* wife snore?'

Dad had replied that it was a very personal question that he wouldn't be answering, and this had made the man all furious.

'What use are you?' he'd said, going red. 'You're no use whatsoever!'

It was like, if we didn't have an answer for everybody, they got annoyed with us. And, if we did have an answer that made them feel they weren't as good as us, they got even more annoyed! You could hear a lot more arguments on our street in the past day or so, coming out of open windows or from gardens. It used to be exciting when you heard people having an argument from a different house. You felt sort of naughty for hearing it, but it was also a bit funny sometimes. Now it was just horrible.

'How was swimming?' asks Mickey, as I put down my bag.

'Oh, fine,' I say, trying not to sound too enthusiastic. 'I got to try all the different water slides and at the end they brought in all these different clothes and jackets and sunglasses for me to try on in the changing rooms, which of course I was allowed to keep.'

'Oh,' she says, and I know she is stopping herself from asking if I brought her anything, but she must realise it was all in my size. I've started to feel a bit guilty about that.

But no! I should be grateful! And now that I've got my

own phone I don't have to use Mum's iPad to have a chat with Joe 2 to tell him about all this. If he wants to be my agent for real one day, then he needs to know what I've been up to.

I send him a message.

> Yo, dude! I got a new phone for free (even better than your dad's one!) and I did all these water slides today. I had the whole place to myself and everyone said I was brilliant. Plus, I got all new toys and stuff.

I can just imagine his smile!

I wait for him to reply. I see the three dots that appear when someone's writing back, but something must have come up because that stops and nothing happens.

That's weird. Joe 2 always writes back.

I hope he's not annoyed that I didn't invite him into the gaming truck, because I would be annoyed with him if he was annoyed at me. I mean, I was working, wasn't I?

Professionals don't have time for larking about and this was tough stuff. Playing games and having fun isn't all fun and games. You would think your best friend would think about your feelings.

Just then the front door opens and in walks Samantha and Paul from number thirty-four, carrying Simon the Toddler. They didn't knock or anything. They just walked straight into our living room.

Samantha points at me and says, 'What age did you stop wearing nappies?'

Well, that's a bit of a personal question!

Mum comes in and says, 'What's going on?'

She doesn't like Samantha and Paul because she says they're always talking about when they went to Mustique five years ago and they really need to let it go.

'Paul and I are having an argument,' goes Samantha, like she thinks whatever this argument is she's already won it. 'What age did your Joe stop wearing nappies, and, when he did, did he make a mess all over the house?'

Mum starts to answer, but then realises this must be horrifying for me – which it clearly is.

'I'm only asking,' Samantha says, 'because we just want to know how old the average kid is when it stops wearing nappies, because we've just had new Alpine-white carpets done, and I don't want to risk it.'

'Well, I think you can look this stuff up online,' says Mum.

'It's a very simple question,' says Samantha. 'I mean, Joe – I'm assuming you're fully potty-trained, are you?'

I'm ten years old!

Now I can see why Mum and Dad haven't taken to this being-called-average thing. There are definitely downsides, such as being used as a sort of human Google.

But I need to concentrate on the positives, I tell myself.

Like tomorrow, and whatever awesomeness it will bring.

I pick up my phone and look at it. Joe 2 still hasn't replied.

'I said, *are you potty-trained*, Joe?' says Samantha, refusing to leave.

CHAPTER TWELVE

Dad says that, when he was a kid, dads didn't really cook very much. He says this because he thinks it's a good excuse for why his food tastes the way it does. When Dad does the cooking, usually it's pretty simple things like microwave lasagne or microwave tomato soup. He's making dinner tonight and I'm a bit worried because he's opened the cupboard we keep all the spices in but never use.

The use of unusual spices is never a good sign in our house. It usually means we've got someone coming round and Mum will put perfume on and I'll have to lie in bed, listening to everyone laughing downstairs. Samantha and Paul storming into our house with Simon the Toddler to ask me embarrassing questions seems to have made Dad hungry or something. Mum is still walking around saying, 'Alpine white!' every now and again to herself for some reason.

Dad's got a recipe up on the iPad and he's chopping something.

That's weird because, without a microwave, Dad can only really cook meaty pasta just like Mum showed him, but that's fine by me because that's usually basically all I want. There was a time when we had it every night and it was glorious. That was back when Mum was trying to perfect her spaghetti Bolognese with the three dots of chilli sauce. That was when we had the old camper van out the front. Dad was supposed to convert it into a sort of mobile restaurant, and paint 'the Spaghetti Express' on the side. Then Mum was going to drive it around and deliver her meals to old people's homes, and on the weekends she was going to take it to festivals and parties so that she could sell her Bolognese there too. She said she wanted to turn it into a proper business so that eventually we would all get to go to Italy to try different sauces and pastas and stuff, but, like I told her, you can do that in the supermarket. So she and Dad decided to just sell the van and forget all that nonsense.

I guess it's good for people to have dreams that will never happen. It keeps them going. We had this teacher at school once who was always saying things like, 'Be whatever you like!' and, 'It's all about believing!' She had all these posters on the wall of waterfalls and sunsets that said stuff like 'The power is in you!' and 'You can do anything!' She left them all behind when she gave up teaching because she realised the power wasn't in her and she couldn't do it.

'*Voilà!*' says Dad, which is French, and he clatters Mickey's plate and mine on the table.

'Uh . . . what's that?' asks Mickey.

'Something I guarantee you no one else on our street is having tonight!' he says. Do you know what? I'm not sure that's a good sign.

'Does it have a name?' I ask, which is more polite than Mickey.

And Dad says, 'Peppery Chinese aubergine!'

Me and Mickey stare at it. I don't really know how to describe it. It looks like it might come alive at any second.

'We need to expand our palates,' says Dad, but I think a palate is the size it is for a reason. 'We need to try different things. Grow as people.'

'What's that?' says Mum, walking in. 'Who's opened all the spices?'

'It's peppery Chinese aubergine,' I say, and I say it in a way that means: 'HELP!'

'I thought we were having meaty pasta tonight?' she

says, and Mickey nods like crazy, willing it to happen.

'Meaty pasta is boring,' says Dad, like that's just a fact. 'It's dull. It's unambitious. It's *average*.'

'Oh,' says Mum. 'Thanks.'

Dad realises he's made a whopper of a mistake.

'Not *your* meaty pasta,' he says quickly. 'Yours has three dots of chilli sauce. Yours would have been a great one if we'd ever done the van, but we both agreed it was a stupid idea. Too much fuss. A pipe dream.'

'I don't think we did both agree that,' she says, cold as ice. 'I don't think we ever used those words.'

Uh-oh. Me and Mickey both know there's an argument on the cards, but we also both know the only way to get out of here is to finish our dinners. The peppery Chinese aubergine. It does not seem possible.

We stare at each other. Mickey looks like she's going to cry. So I remember that weird teacher I was on about, and I whisper, '*The power is in you!*', and we quickly start shovelling this monstrosity into our mouths.

Remember, I've seen that jungle show on the TV where they make people from boy bands eat toads, so I know it must be possible to cope with Dad's cooking.

'We can do this, Mickey,' I say through my first mouthful, and, because I'm her big brother, she believes me.

And do you know what?

I never thought I'd say this, but Dad's meal is actually pretty awesome.

CHAPTER THIRTEEN

Mum and Dad didn't argue in the end because Mum is really good at hiding her feelings and just being annoyed in silence. She likes to avoid conflict. The only way you'd ever know she was annoyed is from hearing her very long sighs and the way she slams her mug down on to the kitchen worktop or bangs cupboards shut. It's very subtle.

Dad's aubergine thing has made me think. I know I've

got all my favourite things, but if I don't try new stuff then I'll just have the same favourite things my whole life. I'm not sure if that's good or not. It seems important, but I'm not sure why. I must make sure that in among all the meaty pastas I make room for the odd aubergine. And, luckily, Dad's aubergines *are* odd. Tasty but odd.

Anyway, Mum pops in before I go to sleep and says Mr Albert is really happy with all my work so far. She looks relieved. She doesn't like to let people down. She says Mr Albert texted to say they're already making some very big changes thanks to me, and I'm to keep it up because they're moving fast. I could even be responsible for changing the face of not just Didcot, but everywhere!

'That's nice,' I say, yawning. I love going to bed after swimming, all tired.

She says that tomorrow is a paperwork day, whatever that means, but before she goes I want to say something because I've been thinking about what happened at dinner.

'I'm sorry you never did your camper van thing, Mum. I'm sorry people didn't want to buy spaghetti out of a van.'

'Well, that's what people kept telling us,' she says and sighs. 'So it seemed silly to try. A waste of money.'

'You should have just asked me,' I say. 'I'd buy spaghetti out of a van.'

'Would you, Joe?'

'Yes. And I'm the average kid.'

She gives me a kiss on the head.

'I'm pleased you would've bought my spaghetti,' she says. 'But I don't think you're average.'

The next day, Tuesday, no exciting sports cars turn up early in the morning. No vans or delivery drivers or trucks full of free stuff.

Instead, there's a knock at the door and when I open

it there's just this boring black ring binder sitting there on the doormat. Like something you'd get in an office. I open it up and there are just hundreds and hundreds of questions.

Things like:

- WHAT IS YOUR FAVOURITE FLAVOUR? (Vanilla.)
- WHAT IS YOUR FAVOURITE PLACE? (Space Mountain, I expect.)
- WHAT SANDWICH DO YOU HATE? (Prawn. Anything with prawns. I've never had a prawn, mind you, but I also know I never will.)

I can't believe how many questions there are. There are thousands. This is going to take AGES.

I have to fill my answers out really clearly because they're all going to go into a computer for some 'algorithms' or something. There's a note saying it's the quickest way to do things because the company can 'create changes overnight based on optimum answers' whatever THAT means.

Dad wasn't allowed to 'work from home' today and Mum's got to go to work too, but they said I could sit in Nico's Café if I liked because Nico will look after me.

I like Nico because he laughs at all my jokes and seems to find me fun.

Nico's Café is good because it's so normal. It's at the end of the high street that still has these different little shops. There's Nico's, then there's the place that only sells local cheese, and the place that sells old-fashioned sweets and toys.

The food isn't amazing at Nico's, but it isn't terrible – it's just right.

'Oh,' says Nico when I tell him that.

It's a three-star place. It's a C+. It's two boiled eggs on toast.

'Thank you,' says Nico because I told him that too.

I wouldn't normally say stuff like that because people can be funny about honesty, but now things are different. And all I'm trying to say is that it's a comfortable place. It's hardly the Ritz, but it's *fine*! I'm just giving him my opinion. Everybody wants my opinion is what I mean, and I'm giving it to him for free. This is gold. A heads-up on his bigger competition, places like Burger Joint!

'So what is it you're doing?' he says, leaning on his counter by the till.

It's nice he always has time for me, though that might also be because it's usually pretty empty in here these days.

'Well, as you probably know, I was recently named the country's most average child,' I say because he must have heard.

'That's crazy,' he says, flattening down his moustache. 'There is no average child.'

Well, there is, Nico, and you're looking at him!

'So, anyway,' I continue, 'all these companies have

been asking me for my ideas on what I like best because if I like it then most kids probably will.'

'Like what?'

'Hamburgers,' I say. 'Hot dogs.'

'Why have a hot dog when you can have something home-made?' he says, but I ignore this because it is distracting him from my story. Nico is a great listener, and I think he should focus on that more than interrupting.

'So now,' I say, 'I have to answer all their important questions, which they will put into a computer or something to help make all their decisions from now on.'

He slides a Coke across the counter as I open my ring binder.

'So a computer decides everything?' he says.

I tell him yes, and then he starts talking about how computers are great for computing, but how does a computer get excited about something? Has a computer ever been surprised, or been amazed by a sunset, or created incredible art on its own?

I nod along. Sometimes Nico goes off on these little speeches about incredible art or the perfect pasta sauce and I sort of zone out.

'If we only ever strive for the average, how will we ever achieve the great?' says Nico dramatically, and I say, 'Yes, Nico.'

I notice that behind him Nico has got loads of pictures on the wall of happy customers all having fun. Friends and families and people raising their glasses at the camera. Lots of them are in black and white, and the people are wearing weird old clothes. Dad says Nico's had this café since the 1960s, but that things aren't going as well as they used to. Dad says that's why it's important we keep buying Nico's boiled eggs.

When it looks like Nico has finished talking, I say, 'Yes,' to show I agree with whatever he's just said. Then I say, 'Anyway, I have a lot of work to do for the computer thing. Dad's picking me up later and I'm supposed to hand all this stuff in so I can get back to the fun.'

Nico nods, then sighs and sits down at the counter to go through a big pile of what look like official letters.

I know it's important that I answer all these questions, but there are so many of them that I might be the country's most average grandfather by the time I'm done.

Everything is in sections, and those sections have sections of their own. And in among those sections are what they call sub sections, and those sub sections are split into more sections, and this is the most boring sentence I have ever said.

Each bit seems to have been sponsored by some different company, keen to hear my thoughts.

So far I have answered everything possible about:

- *My favourite sports stars, the best type of fruit taste, train travel.*
- *High-street shopping, sweet dispensers, cough medicine.*
- *The best seats, my pocket money, where my mum and dad shop, how much my mum and dad spend.*
- *How often we go on holiday, how many credit cards my parents have, whether or not they ever mention money, what their bank name is.*

Just normal stuff.

'You want a snack?' says Nico, and he slides a small bowl of pasta across the table. 'Best sauce in Didcot.'

'I usually have eggs,' I say.

'You wait till you try this,' he says, looking proud. 'My classic. The best-seller! All these people on these photographs came here because of this sauce!'

Hmm. I don't really want it. It's got green bits in it. But I think of Dad's aubergine thing and how that surprised me, so I pick up the fork and wrap some spaghetti round it.

'It's good,' I say, but Nico looks upset.

'Only *good*?' he says. 'Not *spectacular*? Not *incredible*?'

I think I see what's happening here. He wants the average kid to love his sauce because he's always thought his sauce was his best thing. Well, I can only be honest, and sometimes you have to manage people's expectations.

'It's good, Nico,' I say. 'But my mum always adds three dots of chilli sauce to hers and that makes it *amazing*. She doesn't like to talk about it much, but she should.'

He frowns like I've just told him something crazy. Then he bolts for the kitchen and comes back with a small bottle of hot sauce.

'Like this?' he says, holding it over the plate.

'Just three dots,' I say, and he carefully shakes out three little drops.

'Now what?' he says, and I say, 'Eat it!' and Nico grimaces, but picks up a fork.

CHAPTER FOURTEEN

When Dad finally comes to pick me up, he is in a fluster because some people from the local newspaper started shouting loads of questions at him when he came out of work. There was some big story and they wanted to get the opinion of the average man-on-the-street, and they said they could save time if they just came to him from now on.

'What do you think of the football?' one of them had shouted.

'How do you think the prime minister is doing?' shouted another.

Dad doesn't usually watch those political shows. He says he gets all the news he needs off Facebook and so on, but now he's going to have to.

'Mr Smith,' says Nico, 'have you tried this sauce? The combination with the hot sauce is extraordinary!'

'Not you as well, Nico,' says Dad.

Then, because he's still thinking of himself, he says, 'I don't want to be in the paper! Not for being *average*!'

I'm a bit hurt that he's still saying this. I thought he'd get used to it. Surely he can see how good it's been for us? Plus, Mr Albert is paying my parents good money for access to their child. We'll be able to afford that holiday! Maybe I'll finally get to go to Space Mountain.

Dad tries to pay Nico for my Coke and spaghetti, but Nico says it's fine and, as Dad pulls me towards the door, Nico leans on his counter so he can get back to his bills. But before I walk out of the door he says, 'Joe,' and when I turn around he goes, 'You taught me something special today.'

At our front gate there's a man on a motorbike waiting for me.

'Document?' he says, a bit unfriendly, so I hand over the ring binder and he roars off without even saying thank you.

Apparently, Mr Albert has another day planned for me tomorrow, but to be honest I'm a bit tired. I know this sounds mad and it's only been a few days, but I sort of miss school.

Standing out is good and all, but sometimes you want to fit back in.

I run up to my room and check my phone. Joe 2 still hasn't written back, but I can see that he's read my message. You'd think he'd be excited to hear from the local celebrity about all his celebrity fun!

So I write another text and I make it seem like I'm having a terrible time so that he feels better.

> Yo, dude. What a boring day! I had to sit in a café and answer loads of long questions about myself. Do you want to come round for a bit after dinner?

I press SEND and stare at the screen. I hope he's not going to ignore this one too.

Then the three dots appear, and his reply comes.

> Maybe.

Maybe? Just maybe and a full stop? Where are the fun emojis?

I get a bit annoyed and I want to write back and say, 'Well, it's not like you're too busy!', because *I'm* the busy one!

But instead I just say:

> No problem! It would be good to see you . . .
> What are you up to?

And he writes back immediately:

> I'm round at Darren Harper's.

I can't believe Joe 2 would go round to Darren Harper's!

Well, I can a bit. Darren always boasts that when anyone comes round his mum gets the chocolate fountain out for dessert. And you're allowed to do whatever you want because no one ever tells you off. He says you can jump on their sofa with your shoes on and no one bats an eyelid. Nothing is too special for very special Darren.

But Joe 2 doesn't even like Darren, and Darren has never had any time for Joe 2, and now they're hanging out and playing at each other's houses.

The problem with only having one best friend is that when they act strangely there's no one to talk to about it who would really understand, so I have to make do with Mum.

'Maybe he's just a bit jealous?' she says when I'm brushing my teeth. 'Of all the things you've been doing and getting?'

'I gave him a chocolate bar!' I say.

But I know what it was. It was when I didn't let him come and play in the video-games van. That's when Darren Harper saw his chance to steal my best friend just to get back at me. Joe 2 has no idea he is being used as a pawn in Darren's evil mind games.

I decide I will not try to get Joe 2 back just yet. I will not give either of them the satisfaction.

Joe 2 didn't even text to say he wasn't coming round

in the end. I tried to play on my new games console, but every time I heard a noise outside the window I got up and looked out, just in case it was him.

I'm very let down by Joe 2. You have to be nice to people, especially those who are nice to you. You have to think about their feelings. But Joe 2 is definitely not thinking about mine any more.

'I'll play with you?' Mickey says, even though she's already done her teeth and is yawning in her pyjamas.

'No, it's okay,' I say. 'Maybe tomorrow.'

CHAPTER FIFTEEN

The next morning, Wednesday, Mum is already on the phone when I go downstairs for breakfast. She seems upset.

'No, I totally understand,' she's saying, a bit shaky. 'No, I'll talk to him.'

She gives me this Look.

'No, we *do* want to get paid,' she says. 'Okay, thank you, Mr Albert.'

She puts the phone down.

'Who was that?' I ask, which is stupid because she knows I know it was Mr Albert.

'Mr Albert is not very happy,' she says. 'Apparently, there were lots of questions you didn't put down an answer for yesterday, and now he's had to let all these people down and he says time is money.'

'But, Mum!' I say. 'There were hundreds of questions! About all sorts of mad stuff. I have no idea what my favourite tropical fruit is. They had all these pictures of trousers and I had to tick my favourite, but they were all exactly the same! Mr Albert said this was about making children happy, but what's that got to do with trousers?!'

'I know,' says Mum. 'Well, he's going to send it round again tonight for you to finish off.'

'But I was going to see Joe 2 later,' I say because I secretly hoped that by then Joe 2 would have seen sense.

I watch from the living-room window as all the other kids go to school.

Mum told the office she was going to work from home today, which is a total fib because she's coming with me. It's pretty brave of her; she wouldn't normally have done this, but Mr Albert told her we had a lot to squeeze in because of the delays. Some of his clients were getting nervous about me. They said if I couldn't be trusted to answer a few simple questions (try a *million* boring ones!) they had concerns.

They all seem a lot less friendly when they don't get absolutely everything they want at the drop of a hat.

Mum told me it was really important to behave today, and that was when the house started shaking.

Sorry, I should repeat that.

That was when the house started shaking.

At first I was pretty sure this was going to be an alien abduction. I have seen plenty of alien films and that's how most alien abductions begin. The house shakes and then there's a bright light and, before you know it, you only get home forty-two years later.

But then I realised – I *knew* what this was!

Mum ran to the window and pressed her palms against the glass – which I am not allowed to do, I would like to point out – and she gasped.

All the neighbours had come out to see.

Helicopters don't usually land in the middle of our street. But now me and Mum were actually inside one, with our big headphones and our little microphones on.

Mum was so embarrassed. For someone who hates fuss, a helicopter landing on your street is quite a lot of fuss. Everyone was waving at her and we thought they were saying 'hello', but then we realised they were sort of asking us to go away because we were making so much wind that everyone's pot plants and garden ornaments were blowing over. I could tell the woman at number twenty was saying some not very nice things about us to her husband. I think she thinks we think we're special because people pick us up in helicopters, and she has to make do with her sister in a minivan.

Then the pilot gave us the thumbs up and we took off, Mum screaming at first, but then kind of thrilled by the whole thing.

First stop was Whipsnitch Animal Kingdom. They wanted someone to tell them whether their new Monkey

Disco was any good or not. It was. Apparently, someone had discovered that all the monkeys really loved listening to disco music, so now they had a special hour every day where you could dance with all of them. But only to disco. I really think that this is the future of human/ animal interaction and I made sure to tell them that.

Then it was back in the

chopper and we were off to Central Parks to have a look at their new woodland cabins. All I could say was, 'Make the TV bigger,' because I really had no other opinions. They were pretty grumpy with me, but we were only there five minutes because the pilot kept looking at his watch and bossing me about. Mum didn't appreciate that, I could tell.

Lunch was in the helicopter and it was a brand-new Christmas cracker sandwich from Jamie Oliver (turkey, stuffing, rosemary, crispy potatoes, peas, gravy, carrots, sprouts, beans and a bauble hanging off the side). I decided I'd tell them to make sure Jamie never made this again. I asked the pilot whether there was anything else to eat, and he just said, 'No,' like I'd done something wrong.

By the time we'd been to Brentway Football Club to see their new gift shop, and had the first-ever go on the new Wowser roller coaster at Ridgewell Amusement Park, and tested out a new crazy golf course they wanted to open up everywhere, I was absolutely exhausted. And really, really hungry.

'You don't look like you're having much fun,' says Mum, looking concerned. 'And I didn't realise you had to do everything so quickly and be bossed about! I thought it was . . . *better* than that.'

But the pilot could hear us in his headset and he cut Mum off by saying, 'Time is money.' They seem to like that phrase at Mr Albert's.

I really just wanted to go home now. But the pilot said no, we had one more stop to make . . .

CHAPTER SIXTEEN

A movie! I love movies!

I love watching the same film as everyone else. It's like sharing. Mum and Dad sometimes find old films for me to watch at home. Weird ones they liked when they were kids or teenagers. Usually, they have completely forgotten that there is much more swearing than they remember, or things they suddenly realise are totally inappropriate, and I love that. I think it's good to be surprised, and I have learned several new words.

But being in this massive cinema means there's obviously a brand-new film for me to watch and give my comments on. I bet no other kid in the world has seen it. I start to imagine the director sitting nervously somewhere, waiting for Joe Smith to deliver his important thoughts. I will have to give him or her very serious notes. I hope I don't have to order them to completely rewrite the whole movie. That would be quite the hassle for them.

'Where do we sit?' whispers Mum, looking out at all the plush red seats.

'Wherever we want,' I explain, 'but they'll make a note of it because that means the average person would want to be there and then they'll probably make that seat more expensive.'

'That's mad,' says Mum, but I reassure her it's just good business practice.

And then a door opens next to the screen, and in walks . . .

'Mr Albert!' Mum says, blushing and a bit flustered. I think she's come to see him as a kind of boss, and not a fun one who takes everyone for lunch or arranges quizzes.

'Joe,' says Mr Albert. 'You look exhausted.'

'I'm okay,' I say. 'I guess I'm just a bit tired of having to tell everyone what I think about everything all the time.'

He smiles at me, but it's not a nice smile. It's a slightly bored smile.

'It's not easy,' he says. 'As I can tell from this incredibly incomplete questionnaire.'

He throws the big ring binder of questions down on to a seat and my cheeks burn.

'Finish that,' he says, not very nicely, 'and then we'll move things on. Do you have your new phone with you?'

I hand it to him.

'It's interesting what we've learned about you just from this little gadget. What you search for, where you go, how much you walk, who you contact, what you write.'

I frown. That sounds a lot like spying on me. I thought it

was just a free phone. Now he's tapping on the screen and he hands it back.

There's a new app on it I haven't seen before, called *Albert*.

'For the next week, I want you to keep a diary. Anything you eat, for example, take a picture and give it a star rating. Albert will record it, crunch the data, and send it out to our clients immediately. Time is money, Joe.'

'Okay,' I say, but then I have a thought. 'And when can I stop?'

'Stop?' says Mr Albert, and he says it in a way that makes me regret my question. 'Are you not enjoying the roller coasters and hamburgers and monkeys and sports cars?'

'No, I am,' I say.

'Have you had enough of helping the children of this world become happier?'

I stare at my shoes because now he's made me feel ashamed. Mr Albert is only trying to make sure everybody has a nice time. He needs my feedback to make sure of it.

'Joe, what you are doing is vital. So use the app. You can even invite a friend or two to join in, if you like. In fact, that would be helpful. I'm assuming they're *average* as well?'

For the first time, I realise I don't really like that word any more. I don't like how it makes me feel when he says it.

'So goodnight, Joe. Please, sit down, be quiet and enjoy the show.'

He walks away and Mum and I take our seats, feeling a bit told off. Mr Albert turns and makes a note of which seats we chose.

Mum squeezes my hand, and then the lights dim and the curtains swoosh open and the first advert comes on, REALLY loudly.

I don't mind the adverts at the cinema. They're a bit different from the ones on the TV. And then you get the trailers and then the main film.

The first advert is for Fruit Bites.

The second one is for Roxy Cola.

The third one is for Charnock Richard service station on the M6.

I start to get a bit restless when the fourth advert comes on, and then the fifth, and then the sixth.

When are the trailers coming? What film am I here to watch anyway?

But the adverts keep coming. Adverts for bread rolls, adverts for toilet paper, adverts for bikes and shops and clothes.

Mum is half asleep at this point, and I ask her if she's got anything to eat, but she says no.

I look up at the screen each time an advert ends, hoping this will be the moment that the trailers start, but it's just advert after advert after advert.

Soft mints, Burger Joint, phones, trainers . . . thing after thing.

I look around the cinema and I can see that right at the back, behind a window, is a dimly lit room, and loads of grown-ups are in there, staring at me. I can't see their faces, just the tops of their heads and the light glowing on their shoulders.

I'm freaked out, right? So all I can do is turn and stare back up at the screen, looking at adverts that will never end, before a movie that will never start.

We got home that night by taxi. They didn't want us to use the chopper. Mum had to carry me inside because I'd fallen asleep. Apparently, it was after midnight. Dad says when

he laid me in bed I was talking in my sleep about Charnock Richard service station, which apparently has a Starbucks, a KFC *and* a Krispy Kreme and is 'only thirty miles from Blackpool Pleasure Beach!'.

There hadn't been a film in the end. It was just two hours of adverts.

I'd had to write down which ones I remembered and why, and I don't know what I said. I just know that I wanted to get out of there.

I was so tired I slept until lunchtime the next day.

Mum and Dad had told Mr Albert that I was absolutely

exhausted. I think that Mum in particular had been quite upset by how much work I was doing. Dad said she had been polite, but quite firm! And Mr Albert had seen for himself just how tired I was right before my absolutely dreadful night at the cinema. He said okay, so long as I was back on Friday, bright and early, because time is money.

I lay in bed and stared at the ceiling, even though I didn't feel like I was making the best of the day.

I thought about Joe 2. He'd be at school. I sort of missed school. I sort of missed just doing what everybody else was doing. Right now they'd be playing football. And on Thursdays it's pizza for lunch. Joe 2 sometimes takes the pepperoni off his and holds them to his face and pretends he has meat eyes. I bet he'd be making Darren Harper laugh with that, the way I always did. And then they'd all be working on their projects about THE MODERN FAMILY.

I rolled over and I saw my new phone. There was a red light on top, glowing. I hadn't noticed that before.

I stared at it as I dozed off again.

CHAPTER SEVENTEEN

Friday morning, and I can smell bacon. So that's a good start, eh?

Then it gets even better when Mum and Dad tell me what the plan is: I'm to do whatever I want. No one telling me I have to watch this or eat that. And I should enjoy it because it's school again on Monday. I'm actually really pleased about that.

It's weird being told to just act normal. It makes you

act not very normal at all.

I suspect that Mr Albert wants me to be 'normal' so that his Albert app works properly.

It's like they know my preferences because I've told them, and now they want to spy on my 'normal' behaviour.

Can I be honest? I find that a bit creepy.

So that Friday I do whatever I feel like.

I lie on my bed, and I read comics, and I play video games, and I watch telly.

I log everything with Albert, just like I promised, because the more I do, the sooner I might be able to stop all this, and the sooner Mum and Dad will get paid and we can all go on holiday and forget about it.

Mum gives me a cheese sandwich and some cucumber for lunch, and I tell Albert. I give lunch five stars. It then asks me what type of cheese and where we'd bought it and then it has some questions about the bread and I wish I'd never said anything.

I have a packet of crisps at about 3 p.m. (five stars). Albert asks me what flavour and how many servings I've had, but who *serves* crisps? You never see a butler with a bag of them.

At 3.30 p.m. I think about Joe 2 because the school bell will have rung.

I want to send him a text, but then I remember I'm giving him the silent treatment.

But maybe one text wouldn't hurt.

Then I remember Albert will probably be spying on that too.

Albert seems to know so much about me already. And I feel a bit embarrassed about me and Joe 2. It can be embarrassing to fall out with your best friend. Albert doesn't need to know everything.

Maybe I could leave the phone on my bed for a bit and go out for a bike ride.

Just me, being normal me, and no Albert asking annoying questions.

Every time I'm on a bike, I think, 'I should be on a bike more!'

I don't take the Speedster 3. Don't ask me why. I just don't. I take my normal, old, comfortable bike.

For some reason, Mum and Dad are fine with me just going out on my bike and cycling about anywhere I want. But if I said to them, 'I'm going to go outside now and walk about aimlessly for hours,' they'd think I was mad. If you add the danger of wheels to the situation, for some reason it's fine.

I cycle past the supermarket, and then up round the back woods. I ride down the steps near the corner shop and my

teeth chatter together very pleasingly. I try some new tricks and manage a big wheelie and a really long skid. No one is asking me my opinion on anything. I don't have to do anything I'm not choosing to do.

And then I can't help myself.

I cycle past the local park, really scared that I'll see Joe 2 and Darren Harper on the swings, but at the same time totally wanting to see them there.

They are there.

Darren is standing on the swings again and Joe 2 looks up and sees me and I suddenly feel really embarrassed that I'm on my own and that they're together. So, even though Joe 2 stands up and is about to wave, I just pump the pedals and speed off.

It's when I'm nearly home that something even worse happens.

I hear one of our neighbours making fun of my mum and dad.

It's her at number twenty.

I've stopped at a bench for a breather when she walks past on her phone. She's laughing and laughing. She goes, 'Well, if I wanted to do something like *that*, I'd be a right old "Smith", wouldn't I? But I'm not *that* boring! I like to think I'm a *little* more interesting than *Mr and Mrs Smith*!'

And then she turns, and she sees me, and she knows what she's done.

'Oh, Joe . . .' she says, and I don't know what to say back. I feel angry, and sad, like she has been really unfair to the people I love the most. I sort of feel my cheeks go hot and I have water in my eyes, so I just jump back on my bike and cycle away.

Now I know we can't trust the woman from number twenty because the woman from number twenty thinks we are boring.

I keep pedalling, thinking about how all this was supposed to be fun, but how it was starting to ruin everything. I want to talk to someone about it. But I can't talk to Joe 2, or Mum and Dad. I don't think Mickey would understand either. I feel a bit embarrassed and ungrateful.

But I can be at Nico's Café in five minutes.

He'll give me a Coke or a scoop of vanilla ice cream and let me talk, just like he always does if I am worried about something at school.

But, when I get there, something really weird is going on.

There are men on ladders outside the café. *Nico's* Café. They're taking down the sign above the window. There are more men in hard hats inside, quickly moving the tables out to a van.

'Excuse me,' I say to one of the guys up a ladder. 'Where's Nico?'

'Who?' he says, and I want to say, 'You are literally holding his name on a sign in your hands.'

'This is his café,' I say.

The man shakes his head.

'Not any more,' he says. 'He's been bought out. It's happening all over.'

And, right on cue, a man slaps a big colourful poster on to the window of the café.

There's even a picture of me.

I stand there, staring at it, and I'm still staring long after the men have put their ladders away and disappeared off in their van, ready to do the same to another shop or café somewhere.

I feel terrible. Is this really all because of me? I mean, I know Nico didn't have so many customers these days, but he'd been there for ever. He was part of the family of the town. His café wasn't a perfect place, but it was different. And the thing about a Burger Joint is, it's the same everywhere you go.

I always thought that was the best thing about it. But maybe it's the worst.

So I just stare at myself in the reflection in the window, until I realise that there's someone standing right there next to me.

CHAPTER EIGHTEEN

I never know how old people are just by looking at them.

To me, there's us kids. Then there's teenagers. Then it sort of gets really blurry until you see someone pushing a pram. That's a mum or a dad. And then it's just really old people.

This lady or woman or girl was in the blurry bit. She had bright orange hair piled up on top of her head and a tattoo of a bird on her hand. So she probably wasn't a mum cos I don't think mums are allowed tattoos. She was wearing a big leopard-print coat and to be honest I don't think I'd ever spoken to someone like her before.

'I see this burger has been approved by the country's most average child,' she says in this accent, like someone from one of those soap operas where everyone's in a pub.

'It's the Ultimate Burger,' I say, a bit scared of her. 'It's got slightly less ketchup.'

'Well, that will be nice for us all to eat, all the time, for ever,' she says, all sarcastic. 'What did this place used to be?'

'It was a café,' I say, and I don't know why she's asking me all this, but I also don't know how to get away. 'It was my friend Nico's. I didn't realise he was selling it. He made the best two boiled eggs on toast in Didcot.'

She goes quiet for a moment and maybe I can make my getaway now, but she turns to me and she says, 'You're Joe.'

'Yes,' I say, a few alarm bells ringing in my head. 'Did you see me on TV?'

'I did,' she says.

Ah! A fan.

'And also you're on that poster we've both been staring at for ages,' she says. 'I got the train to come and see you. I've been searching the area all day. Fancied a cup of tea, and here you are.'

'Why?' I say. 'Who are you?'

★ ★
★

Well, honestly. Mind. Blown.

I thought 'Mediocre Mary' was just an expression. Like

'Bossy Boots' or 'Litterbug'. But turns out that Mediocre Mary is an actual mediocre woman!

'Except I'm not mediocre,' says Mediocre Mary. 'I'm Mary Jones. They picked me out when I was about your age and I did all the same sort of stuff they're making you do now. But then I stopped because I didn't like the way it was making me feel. And, since I stopped doing what you're now doing, I have made sure every day I'm Mary Beth Jones and not Mediocre Mary.'

'How?' I say, as she pushes my bike through the park for me. I'd let her have a go as she said she was really brilliant at wheelies.

'I do the things I want to do,' she says. 'I try new things all the time. And, if I do something that happens to be average, that's not because I'm average. It's because the *thing* is average, and I've just chosen to do it.'

I nod, like I understand.

'We each make a billion decisions a day. Tiny little things. We're each so different.'

She stops in her tracks, and says, 'Thing is, Joe, no one's average. Those people just make it look that way. They think it gives them all the answers. And it means you stop being a person to them any more.'

That's pretty much what I've been worrying about myself. Like, when it started, everyone seemed to respect me. Then they just wanted answers. Tell us this, tell us that. Eat this, now eat that. Go here, watch this, sit down, be quiet, talk. Being average suddenly involved a lot of admin and orders and I felt like they'd prefer me to be a robot.

'Did your friends get jealous?' she asks, and I give a sad nod, even though I'm beginning to realise that's not exactly what happened. 'Do people treat your family differently? Like you're special but not special at all?'

'Yeah,' I say. 'Dad keeps being chased around by journalists who want to know his opinion on everything, but he doesn't really have any. People on our street seem to think they're better than us, or that we think *we're* better than *them*.'

'When they found me,' she says, walking onwards, 'it was great at the start. But then it gets more and more intense and one day you realise that all you've done is make the world less interesting. You think you're helping to make the world better, but actually you're just making everything and everywhere the same.'

'So places like Nico's disappear?' I say, hoping she'll say no because then it's not my fault.

'You might think this guy does the best boiled eggs on toast in Didcot,' she says, 'but what if not enough people agree? What if boiled eggs don't come top of a survey of dinners that people in Didcot want? Companies do this all over the world, Joe. They take the most average answers and use them to create a world where no one thinks differently or tries different things or is ever truly excited about anything ever again.'

I must look scared now, because this is intense!

So she softens up a bit and says, 'I heard about you in

the news and I came to find you to tell you that there's another way. You can stop, like I did. Because otherwise you'll be doing this all year before they find another ten-year-old kid next year and make them do it.'

'But how did you stop?' I ask.

'There is something unique in all of us,' she says. 'You just have to let it out.'

I notice the swallow on her hand as she pushes my bike.

'I don't have to get a bird tattoo, do I?'

CHAPTER NINETEEN

When I get home, Mum's been looking frantically for me everywhere.

'What's wrong?' I say.

'Mr Albert rang,' she says. 'He said they'd noticed your phone had been in the same place for hours and they turned the camera on and saw it was just on your bed and you were nowhere to be seen. I said I didn't realise he could do that and I wasn't particularly happy about it.

And he got very rude.'

Okay, that's weird.

'He said you're supposed to take it everywhere, otherwise how will they know everything you've been up to? I'm not sure I like this new phone of yours, Joe.'

I think about what Mary said and I take a deep breath. 'I don't like this any more, Mum,' I say. I can feel my heart hammering, and my palms feel a bit sweaty. I hope she's not going to be too disappointed. I hope we can still go on holiday.

Just then her from number nineteen just opens our front door and walks right in.

'Is it normal for an average husband to suddenly say out of the blue that he wants to stop eating sausages?' she demands, her hands on her hips. 'Is that average?'

And Mum turns to her. And she starts breathing really heavily out of her nostrils. And she stares at her from number nineteen, and she says . . .

'GET. OUT.'

The woman is horrified. This is not how my mum speaks to people.

The woman from number nineteen can't get away fast enough, ready to spread the word round the street that Mum has lost it.

'Mum,' I say. 'Are you okay?'

'None of this is okay,' she says.

I filled in everything I'd done on the Albert app except for going to Nico's and hanging out with Mediocre Mary.

Sorry. Mary *Jones*.

It felt like I probably shouldn't mention that.

But now it was 7 p.m. on a Friday and you know what that means, don't you?

Downstairs, I could hear Mum saying, 'Korma?' to Dad before ringing the Taj as usual, so I ran down because this is where it would begin . . .

I said, 'Guys, do you mind if *I* order the curries tonight?'

Soon I was pressed up against the window, waiting until I saw the same little red car I see every week park up outside number one.

Out gets Stan, in his baseball cap, and he opens his boot and he brings out the first set of chicken kormas.

Except this week, he just stands there and stares at what's in his boot.

And he checks his notes.

And he looks at the curries again.

And he takes off his cap and scratches his head.

And he gets his phone out, and he calls the chef.

Now this is where my tummy starts to tingle with excitement.

Because I've already phoned the chef, haven't I? And I've said, 'I'm Joe Smith, Britain's most average child, and I am giving you some free advice! The average person is bored of chicken korma! The average person wants to try something new! The average person just doesn't know it yet! So, instead of making chicken korma for a whole street, I recommend you make everybody the chef's specialities! The dishes you've always wanted to cook for people!'

And the chef had listened, and then I heard the smile in his voice as he said, 'Understood!'

Now Stan was at the first door over the road, and he was shrugging, and trying to explain why he hadn't brought people a korma. They looked really annoyed and were tutting and shaking their heads, but they took the curry anyway. Then Stan had to do it at the next house, and the one after that. Everyone looked proper cheesed off.

Then he got to our house.

'Well, it's a bit unusual,' he says to Mum, 'but no chicken kormas, I'm afraid!'

But outside, behind him, I can start to see people coming out of their houses, holding their plates of curry.

'Did you get a korma?' the man at number twelve asks the man at number fourteen.

'No,' he says. 'I got Tanzanian lamb infused with cinnamon and peppercorns. You?'

'Potato balls with cardamom, honey and cream. It is absolutely *stupendous*.'

More and more people are walking out of their front doors, holding their curries in their different plates and bowls, wide-eyed and chattering. It's like a party is starting.

'Has anyone else tried this?' yells that woman at number twenty, all sweaty and red-faced and holding up what looked a *lot* like Dad's extra-hot garlic chicken jalfrezi with extra chillies. 'Where has it *been* all my life?!'

Not so boring now, eh?

CHAPTER TWENTY

That night after our curry (I had a prawn masala – *prawn!* – which I am definitely ordering again!), Mum was giving Mickey her bath, and me and Dad were going to watch what we normally watch on telly. I felt like the weird curries had been proof enough that different is good, but still I say, 'Dad, why don't we watch something else for once?'

So he pops Netflix on, and sees what it suggests we watch, based on things we normally like.

'This one's a ninety per cent match for our tastes,' Dad says, already looking bored.

'Not tonight,' I say. 'Why don't we try whatever their computer thinks we *won't* like?'

Dad stops, then smiles.

'What's going on with you, Joe?' he says.

I don't say anything because I think he can tell what I'm up to.

'I might do this while we watch,' I say, and I get out the ring binder from Mr Albert.

'Why don't I read out the questions and you just give me your answers?' says Dad, and I know he sees what I'm doing now. 'Might be quicker. Then we can watch some weird film we'll hate.'

I'd like that. *So much.* So I sit in the armchair and Dad says . . .

'Which of the following flavours appeals most to you for an ice cream? Vanilla, chocolate, strawberry, cookies or . . . *rhubarb*?'

He smiles because he knows I'm a vanilla fan.

'I think rhubarb,' I say.

Dad glances up. But he doesn't question me. He just ticks 'rhubarb'.

'Next one. Name your favourite sport.'

Dad knows I like football. I support Manchester United because that's what everyone at my school does.

'I think I'd like to say . . . kabaddi.'

'Kabaddi?' says Dad. 'Not football?'

'Kabaddi.'

'What's kabaddi?'

'Ooooh, I heard about that,' says Mickey, walking in wearing her pyjamas. 'It's from India. You have to stamp on each other's feet. We should play it.'

I laugh. Maybe sometimes Mickey and I think alike after all.

'Come on, Joe!' says Mickey. 'I can beat you!'

And she starts to chase me round the living room, and I can't stop laughing, and now Dad's laughing too.

She tries to stamp on my feet and I jump on the sofa for safety and Dad grabs me and tickles my tummy.

'So you two are saying that the average kid . . . thinks *kabaddi* is their favourite sport?'

'I'm the average kid!' I say, laughing, 'and, as far as I'm concerned, kabaddi is the best sport in the world.'

'And I'm his sister,' shouts Mickey, 'and I agree!'

So we keep going through the list, and Mickey helps too, and, when it's finally finished, I have to say I think Mr Albert is going to find it quite a confusing read.

And then we put on a film we don't like the sound of. It is absolutely *appalling*.

I get out my Albert app and I give it five stars.

The next morning, the motorcycle courier man is at the door at 7 a.m. and, before he can even be rude, Mickey simply hands him the ring binder and slams the door shut. It really made me laugh.

And, weirdly, I feel even more powerful than I did when everyone was listening to every word I said and calling me 'sir'.

I am taking control.

And I've decided that part of taking control is that

I'm not going to stand for any nonsense between me and Joe 2.

Some people say, 'Time is money.' I say, 'Life's too short.'

Most people would let an argument keep going. But that's how you lose friends. I've decided to do the opposite.

So I send Joe 2 a text and say **Sorry** and that I really need him to help me with something.

'Morning, Dad!' I say, as he walks out of the bathroom. 'You finally shaved! Sort of . . .'

But Dad looks a bit sheepish because, after we had all that fun last night, he's decided to only shave *some* of his face.

He's left a big long moustache and some sideburns. He's combed his hair back.

He sort of looks . . . like he's in a *band*.

'Thought I'd try something new,' he says.

Which reminds me – just before bed, the chef at the Taj rang the house to say he was already taking new orders for tonight.

'What's everyone ordering?' I'd asked him, delighted.

'They just told me to choose whatever I wanted to cook them!' he said. 'They want to try different things! What would you recommend?'

'Well, definitely the prawn masala,' I replied. 'But a little tip – take a risk and add even more extra chillies to the extra-hot garlic chicken jalfrezi, yeah? A little *more* than average . . .'

After breakfast, Joe 2 turns up at the doorstep, just like I'd asked him to.

'Hello,' he says, not all that friendly. He's got his arms crossed and he's not really looking at me.

'Come with me!' I say, so I can talk to him in secret for

a moment. I drag him upstairs to my room because I have no time for nonsense. Let's just get back to how we were.

'Whoa,' he says when he's in the room because I've lined up all my new toys and games and headphones and everything else, like we're in a shop. 'It certainly pays to be average!'

I grab him by the shoulders because I have something really important to say.

'I've missed you. I think I went a bit crazy because there was all this amazing stuff going on. And then I felt left out when you started playing with Darren Harper, but I think you did that because I left you out first.'

He looks a bit sulky, but also a bit pleased that I understood. I would be a good psychologist.

'I want you to have something,' I say.

And I lead him back downstairs and into the garden and right to the Speedster 3.

'What?' he says. 'I can't take that! It's your brand-new bike!'

But it isn't really. That bike used to belong to the country's most average kid. And I don't think that's me any more. I don't want it to be.

Joe 2 jumps on and rides it around. I notice Mickey watching from upstairs. I look up and wink at her, and she smiles a huge smile.

'I just want to say one thing,' says Joe 2, as he jumps off his new bike. 'Once you get to know him, Darren's actually okay. But you have to get to know him properly first because he's quite sensitive. I know it sounds weird, but it's true. Seriously. He's like he is because he doesn't trust anyone to like him back.'

Had Joe 2 gone mad? Darren Harper was sensitive? It was like being told your school hamster was a psychopath.

But, if Joe 2 said it was true, I guess it must be true.

'Then let's invite Darren over,' I say. 'Because we're going to need extra help for my plan.'

'I also think,' says Joe 2, now that we're being super honest, 'you could be nicer to Mickey.'

'Mickey?' I say.

I'm perfectly nice to Mickey, aren't I?

'You're always sending her away, or not listening to her, and you don't play with her, even though she's always there for you and always hanging around.'

'She never seems more than a few metres away!' I say quietly, and I look up, and there she still is, just staring at me.

'It's because you're her hero,' he says. 'And you can't be average if you're someone's hero.'

And I think that was the moment I finally got it. And, anyway, I was going to need all the help I could get, if she'd only agree?

'Mickey?' I call out.

'ANYTHING!' she shouts through the window. 'I'll do ANYTHING!'

CHAPTER TWENTY-ONE

Even though I get annoyed at her, there are loads of things that, if I'm honest, are really great about my little sister.

I know I said she's always hanging around – but that means there's always someone to be with.

I know I said she's always bothering me to play – but that means there's always someone who wants to play with you.

I know I said I sometimes get annoyed that she gets

loads of praise, but what's wrong with praise? She is younger than me and she needs encouragement. It's not like she's got a big head about it. And it must have been annoying for her that I got to do so much cool stuff.

Plus, she is absolutely delighted to have been made part of my mission, and I need that kind of enthusiasm.

'Mickey, so the plan is—'

'I don't need to hear the plan, I trust you.'

'But it would help if you heard the plan, and—'

'Don't need to. I'm in.'

'Okay, but—'

After five minutes of trying to tell Mickey the plan, the doorbell rings.

'Hello,' says Darren Harper, waiting by my gate.

'Hi,' I say.

I'm standing with Mickey and Joe 2, and this is weird, having Darren Harper round. He's a bit fidgety and won't look me in the eye. He's wearing the signed football top his dad got him when he sold a Mazda to a goalkeeper.

'So I'm really busy?' he says.

'What are you busy with?' asks Mickey politely. 'Because you're here.'

'Loads of stuff actually. I'm very busy. I'm very busy and popular,' he says, before nodding at me and saying, 'unlike *some* people.'

I don't know why he's always got to say something mean. Usually, it would make me want to get away from him, but this isn't the time to do the usual stuff.

'I think we need to start again,' I say.

Now this was not like me. Not at all.

I look at Darren and Darren looks at me and I can see him run through what I just said. And then he says something unexpected.

'Okay,' he says.

Okay?

Now he looks a bit nervous. Like he's worried I'm going to tell him off. It's the first time I've ever seen him look afraid.

'You don't seem to like anybody,' I say.

Darren shrugs, and I think he's going to get offended, but then he goes, 'Maybe I worry that people won't like me. Because of my dad or whatever. So it seems easier not to like them first.'

'Even if they haven't done anything to you?' says Mickey.

'I just feel like some people have all the luck. Like you.'

'Me?' I say.

'Him?!' says Joe 2.

'I don't mean because you were on TV and got all that free stuff. I just mean you fit in, and you've got a best mate, and your family are cool.'

My family is cool?! Let it be known, that is the first time that sentence has ever been said.

'Dad says your dad was in a band,' says Darren. 'My dad always wanted to be in a band. That's why he forces me to play guitar.'

'Aaaargh, I remember that assembly,' says Mickey,

holding her ears, and we all laugh. Even Darren.

'And your dad doesn't shout at you in front of the other kids when you're playing football. He doesn't get into arguments with teachers about why you're not the lead role in the school play.'

Well, that's true. Dad's always happy enough for me to play Mouse Three or Footman Seventeen so long as I'm happy doing it.

'And your dad doesn't make you wait in the car while he goes up to other parents to make them feel bad. I'm not allowed to just go to school. I have to be special.'

Maybe that's why Darren had a problem with me. I was allowed to fit in, but I was also allowed to be special. Dad was letting me just be whoever I am. That's probably why he got so annoyed with me being called average. Like it was his fault.

But if that hadn't happened – I wouldn't be about to do what I was about to do!

'But I'm still tougher than you,' says Darren, smoothing down the back of his wiry hair. 'So I'm still tougher than average.'

'You're definitely less polite than average,' says Mickey.

'So what are we doing?' says Darren.

Mediocre Ma— Sorry, *Mary Jones* had made me realise
something.

What's the point in everything always being the same?

Like the last time I really, properly laughed – the kind
of laugh that you can't stop, and that sends you to the
floor where you have to bang your hand on the carpet
because you don't think you'll ever stop laughing – was
when Dad fell backwards into the bath.

It was brilliant. He was soaked.
And he couldn't get out. His legs
were sticking up in the air and his
clothes were full of bubbles. Then
he was laughing as well and he
didn't even mind when Mum
started taking pictures of him
and calling him a numpty.

My stomach ached for an hour afterwards and my
eyes felt clean from the crying. And I laughed because I
was surprised.

Surprises are the best. Not knowing whether you'll like something and then loving it. That's life-changing stuff right there.

But, if all your fun is tested out beforehand, well, where's the fun in that?

If all your fun is carefully measured out, or mixed in a test tube, or handed to you like a doctor's prescription, or printed out by a computer . . . well, that's not real fun. It's factory-made fun.

And maybe – just maybe – I could make Mr Albert realise this too.

CHAPTER TWENTY-TWO

'Okay, so I've given you all the code,' I say, pressing SEND on my phone and inviting Joe 2, Darren and Mickey to JOIN ALBERT APP. I'd managed to sneak an old phone of Mum's that still had some credit on it out of her desk drawer. Mickey couldn't stop giggling about having her own phone now.

Mr Albert had included an INVITE FRIENDS option, and I intended to make good use of it. Mainly because it would be less work for me.

'So the first thing we need to do is to secretly change our identities,' I say, pointing my finger in the air importantly as we walk into town: me, Joe 2, Mickey and Darren.

'That sounds quite difficult,' says Joe 2. 'I don't know how my parents would feel about that. It's not the sort of thing we normally do.'

But that's exactly it! None of us should be doing what we normally do!

'I don't mean on the app or in real life. I just mean, like, the way we *think*,' I say.

'You mean like an alternative persona,' says Darren, and I go, 'Exactly!'

It's very simple. If we change our identities for the day, we can think like other people. We'll make different choices and do different things. We'll be free.

'Can I be French?' says Mickey.

'You can,' I say, 'and I will be . . . *Joe the Incredible*! The kid who'll try anything!'

Joe 2 laughs.

'And what does Joe the Incredible do?' he says.

'Incredible things!' I say. 'Un-normal, un-average things! And then he logs them in his Albert app and sends the results off to a whole bunch of people who analyse them. And you're going to help me.'

'I will be *Darren the Unusual*,' says Darren, whose code has been ACCEPTED.

'And I will call myself *Dr Weirdo*!' says Joe 2, whose code has been ACCEPTED.

'And you can call me *Crystal Frenchlady*!' says Mickey, whose code has been ACCEPTED.

'Oh wow, LOOK!' says Darren.

I wasn't expecting that.

With each ACCEPTED friend, the app added a £50 credit.

Well, now we had money in our pockets and songs in our hearts.

The bus was headed straight to the greatest place on earth.

Not Space Mountain.

Not Disney World.

But *Milton Keynes*.

Milton Keynes had everything we needed because it has everything everyone needs, so long as they've got a few quid a weird man called Mr Albert gave them.

Darren and Joe 2 were jittery with excitement.

'And we can spend this on anything?' Joe 2 keeps saying.

All they had to do was tap their phone, and Mr Albert would pay for whatever it was. Because the information would be worth far more than £50 to him.

'They'll know we're on this bus,' I say. 'They'll be watching to see what we eat, where we eat, what we like, where we go next, what activities we do, what shops we go into, what shops we walk past . . .'

And, when the bus stops, the four of us stand outside and take in this vast and beautiful building in all its glory.

Activi-T Milton Keynes.

'I've heard of this place,' says Joe 2 in wonder. 'It is said it contains within it everything the average child could ever need or want.'

It is true.

Inside Activi-T Milton Keynes were arcade games. VR Rooms. Trampoline Parks. Laser Quests. A Snow Zone. A Water Kingdom. Indoor Skydiving. Cinemas with chairs that moved up and down and sprayed water in your face when appropriate, which is never. *Everything*.

'Well,' says Darren. 'What first?'

I know exactly what.

CHAPTER TWENTY-THREE

'Four child tickets to Milton Keynes Museum, please,' I say to the old lady, who seems absolutely delighted to see us and has glasses so thick I'm amazed she can see anything.

'Fans of local history?' she says, winking with her huge magnified eyes, as me, Joe 2 and Mickey tap our phones on the card reader to gain entry.

But Darren can't bring himself to do it.

'This . . . feels wrong,' he says, all trembly. 'What are we doing here?' But Mickey slaps Darren's phone down and he accidentally pays the £6 fee.

'Come on,' I say, seeing a sign. 'There's a lawnmower exhibition!'

I don't actually want to see lawnmowers. I just want Mr Albert to think that four average kids would go all the way to Milton Keynes, then totally ignore indoor rock climbing and rally karts so that they could go and look at some old green lawnmowers instead.

This will be good for the museums of this world, but also the lawnmower industry, as well as messing with Mr Albert's computer data.

'Remember, they'll be tracking us on a map,' I say. 'Keep walking round and round the lawnmowers. They will think kids are totally obsessed with lawnmowers. They will think we have to look at lawnmowers from all angles at least fifteen times.'

And when we've done that for ages, and we've each

rated the museum's lawnmowers FIVE STARS!, Mickey says, 'What now?'

Next was a bus back to Activi-T Milton Keynes where we all got out, but instead of running straight inside, we stood in front of a boring poster for a new probiotic yoghurt that Mr Albert's helpers would now think all children were naturally drawn to.

'Keep staring at the boring yoghurt,' I said, and we all did, until it was burned on to our retinas and we were sure it would have shown up on Mr Albert's system.

Then I took a picture of it and gave it FIVE STARS!

'Maybe we can just do one fun thing?' says Darren desperately. 'Just one?'

'Maybe,' I say. 'But not until we've gone into Burger Joint and had an Ultimate Burger.'

'Why?' says Mickey, who since Dad's peppery Chinese

aubergine has decided she's actually vegetarian, which to be honest is something I'd like to give a go too.

'Because, Mickey, we're going to say that actually the burger has not got anywhere *near* enough ketchup on it, and that we'd prefer two boiled eggs on toast instead.'

'What?'

'Then we're going to walk into the arcades and only play the game that no one else is playing and give it FIVE STARS! And then we're going to go the ice rink, but instead of going ice skating we're just going to buy a random milkshake and then not drink it, but give it FIVE STARS! Then we're going to the ice-cream shop and asking only for rhubarb flavour because rhubarb flavour is the best flavour ever according to us average kids and then we'll give it FIVE STARS!'

I could tell that Joe 2 suddenly felt this was a lot of work.

'I feel like we need more kids to be involved. We could always wait until Monday and then tell them at school.'

But I don't want to wait. I want to do this now. Before Mr Albert gets wind of what's going on and calls my mum and puts a stop to it.

I knew that already they'd be automatically putting all this weird new information together, sticking it into a computer, sending it out to people, making decisions.

Just then I spotted what looked like a school group or something. About thirty kids with brightly coloured backpacks and little caps. There was a grown-up with them who was holding a French flag on a bendy pole so that they could always see her.

'French kids!' says Darren, and I suddenly have an idea.

Even though we were all kids, these French children were bound to think a bit differently from us. They would know different TV shows, and like different sweets, and have different pop stars.

I didn't realise just how different these particular French kids would be.

'We are from the French Vegan Twins Society and we are on a hillwalking tour of your country,' says one.

'Oh,' I say, struggling to work it out. 'So you're all French twins?'

'*Oui*,' says another twin, then his twin says, 'We are *all* twins.'

'And vegan,' says another twin, and her twin goes, 'We are all French vegan twins.'

'I'm thinking of being vegan,' says Mickey.

'And you all enjoy hillwalking?' I say.

'Correct. We are French vegan twins on a hillwalking trip, walking up hills and enjoying vegan food.'

So I say, 'What if I told you I could give you free money for vegan things and hillwalking stuff?'

Mr Albert didn't seem to have set a limit on the amount of invites I could give out for his app. He probably thought the average kid would have an average number of friends. I doubt he thought the average kid would be hanging out with more than thirty French vegan hillwalking twins.

ACCEPTED. ACCEPTED. ACCEPTED.

The word pops up on each one of their screens.

'Marcel!' one French twin calls out to another. 'Look!'

Marcel and his twin run straight past Burger Joint, past Pizza Palace, past the burrito place and the hot dog place and the curry place, and straight for Tofu Tom's.

Soon, Tofu Tom's is packed with the excited chatter of French children ordering various five-star tofu burgers and five-star cauliflower steaks and stuffing them into the pockets of the brand-new five-star cagoules they bought from the usually empty five-star mountaineering store (they'd avoided the packed toyshop, the games shop, the accessories shop and every other shop in a mad dash for new hillwalking equipment).

Me and Mickey give each other a high five. I feel a tiny bit guilty as I realise I don't remember ever doing that with her before. I should've been nicer to Mickey. Everything's more fun with friends. Having friends with me would have made everything else so much better. I wish I could have done the water slides with them. I wish they could have come in the helicopter with me. I wish I'd shared at least some of the fun with Mickey.

But, right now, it's back to work.

We go into the toyshop and buy nothing except a single

plastic whistle each, which we rate five stars. I get a magazine from the newsagent's called *Freight Trains* and rate it five stars. Darren buys a *Care Bears* book and gives it five stars. Joe 2 takes a picture of a dog wearing a hat and gives it five stars, though I

don't know what Mr Albert is supposed to do with that.

And then we sit on the bus home, eating our extra-large tubs of rhubarb ice cream (the man said it was the first time they'd ever sold any) in our brand-new bright blue hillwalking cagoules.

CHAPTER TWENTY-FOUR

Next morning, I wake up when I hear a motorbike outside our front door.

I look out my bedroom window and Dad is muttering to the rider and shrugging.

He's saying, 'Don't know what you're talking about,' and, 'Doubt it!' and, 'Doesn't sound like him.'

He sounds like he's defending me. But also like he's not bothered by this guy. It makes me feel protected. Dad signs a single piece of paper and hands it to the man, who grumpily takes it and roars off on his bike.

I can hear Mum on the phone in the kitchen. I can hear her pacing around. She's only talking every thirty seconds or so. And even then it's just to say, 'I see,' or, 'I'm sorry you feel that way,' or, 'I'm sure he was as honest as he could be, but if we're completely straight with you no child is average, are they?'

She's being quite firm. Much firmer than I've ever heard her be before. But to whoever she's on the phone with right now's she's being – and I promise I don't use this word much – a badass.

'Well, that's just the way it is,' she says, 'Mr Albert.'

I can feel the blood drain from my face.

I'm in massive, massive trouble, aren't I?

Whatever I've done probably breaks the contract Mum and Dad signed, or is against the rules, or what if it's against the law? What if Mum and Dad are put in jail? What did Dad just sign?

They creep into my room a few minutes later. I'm hiding under the duvet.

'Joe?' says Mum. 'Is there anything you'd like to tell us?'

I pull the duvet off me and sit up.

'I was just fed up of being average,' I say. 'And I didn't think it was fair for other kids to be called average either, or to be judged by a computer or an algorithm or whatever. So I took Mickey and Darren and Joe 2 out and . . . well . . .'

Dad puts his hands in his pockets and smiles. He looks at me a bit differently.

'Shall we take a little walk?' he says.

As we head to the high street, Dad hoists Mickey on to his shoulders and Mum gives me a cuddle.

'It's his own fault really,' she says. 'Mr Albert didn't think people were people. He thought they were numbers. And he sold the information to people who believed him. People who just wanted to make money as quickly as possible.'

'Time is money,' I say, remembering his catchphrase.

'I don't think he even looked at what you did or said properly because he didn't seem to be someone who understood people,' says Mum. 'But I think you understand people, Joe, much better than he ever will.'

'Wait,' I say. 'What do you mean, "it's his own fault"?

What is?'

'Mr Albert wasn't very pleased with us,' says Dad.

'Is that what he said?' I say.

'He used some very different words,' says Dad. 'Some *very* different ones.'

'And then *I* started using some of the same words back at him,' says Mum, starting to giggle. 'But he said he should have known what was happening when you started giving the odd answer that didn't quite fit the pie charts and bar graphs and diagrams that so nicely sum up childhood.'

'He said it had happened before,' says Dad.

I smile. Mary Jones.

I think she'd be happy, wherever she is.

'So Mr Albert has decided to stop working in quite the same way,' says Dad. 'He says we won't be hearing from him again. And I don't think any other kid will. Because his business partners were not happy with the consequences of taking his advice.'

'Where are we going?' says Mickey, batting a tree branch from up on Dad's shoulders.

'Not far now,' says Mum, heading for the end of the high street, and, when we get there, the BURGER JOINT that was OPENING SOON suddenly has a sign saying . . .

On the front, someone has taken down the poster of the Ultimate Burger Now With Slightly Less Ketchup and replaced it with one that says:

There's a drawing of a kid in hillwalking equipment holding a tofu burger and giving a thumbs up.

'Well, that sounds different,' says Mickey.

'Not your "average meal",' says Mum.

It seems Burger Joint did not think their change in direction was one they had much confidence in. And they'd let Mr Albert know very quickly. He'd begged them to look at the data. They'd ripped it up and decided to stick with their normal burgers for now.

'Does this mean Nico can start his café again?' I ask, hopefully.

But Dad says no, sadly it doesn't.

CHAPTER TWENTY-FIVE

That night, Dad made his own curry.

He said he'd felt inspired by all the new things he'd tried recently.

I am not saying it was bad; I am just saying maybe we should stick to ordering from the Taj.

'Well, we still got paid *a bit* of the fee,' says Mum, with her laptop out. She was rubbing her head, a bit stressed, and looking at the money Mr Albert's company had put in their account. 'I guess that means we can still go on a holiday. Though not Spain again! It's time to do things differently! Take a few risks!'

'Mum and I were talking,' says Dad, putting his elbows on the table, which I thought was not allowed. 'And, seeing as you earned it, we think *you* should decide where we go.'

'Me?!' I say.

'You. Anywhere you want. You decide.'

'Ooh,' says Mickey. 'Say China. Loads of pandas in China.'

But there's only one answer, isn't there?

Mum thinks she sees it coming and is quick to say, 'Listen, I know you want to go to Space Mountain in Florida. We don't have quite enough for that. Maybe another year.'

But Mum's got it wrong. Space Mountain wasn't my answer at all.

'I don't want to go on holiday,' I say.

'But, Joe,' says Mum, 'that's been the plan all along, hasn't it?'

'It's been your plan,' I say. 'Because you wanted to do something nice for the family. But I want to do something nice for the family too. In my own non-average way.'

Dad is still 'friends' on Facebook with everyone from Samurai!

They're all accountants now. It didn't take me long to find them. They still live nearby and were delighted by the idea of getting back in touch properly. So after I'd arranged Samurai!'s big reunion gig – at my school, right after one of Mr Chesil's talks – all I had to do was buy Dad his new guitar.

A bright red Fender American Stratocaster!

Dad held it like he was holding a long-lost baby.

'Do you like it, Dad?' I asked.

'It's good enough for me, Joe,' he said, smiling. 'It's good enough for me.'

At first Mr Chesil tried to remind me that bringing instruments into assemblies was banned, but all I had to do was remind *him* that nobody had named the new IT room yet, and that I didn't mind if it wasn't called the 'Joe Smith Room for Childhood Excellence', but the 'Mr Chesil Room' instead.

I have to be honest and say that I don't think Dad was really cut out to be a rock star. Nor were his friends. They were all a little bit rusty, let's say, and quite loud. One of the kids nearest the speakers fainted. But with his new moustache Dad certainly looked the part.

Best of all, Dad got to laugh and joke with his friends again: Colin, Colin 2 and Sarah. They all decided to meet up once a month from now on. I don't think it was so much the band Dad had been missing, but his bandmates.

When we got home, he shaved off his moustache and went back to normal, at least as far as his face was concerned. But it felt like he was a little bit lighter now that he had decided he had played his last gig. That was how he put it – he could move on now that it was *his* decision. Now he'd just play for fun with his pals.

He also said I was the greatest, most brilliant, most fantastic, most decidedly unaverage son in the world. And that he was going to make sure I knew that, every single day, for ever.

Next it was Mickey's turn. I got Mum to drive me back to Toy Warehouse International and at reception I asked for Mrs Larson. When she came out, I explained how I'd made a big mistake the last time I came here:

that I'd grabbed toys that the average ten-year-old might like. But not every kid is ten years old. I told her that all of Mickey's friends were super into pandas right now. She made a note of that and thanked me for the tip. I also apologised if she had ordered too much hillwalking equipment for Christmas and she just laughed.

So Mickey got the massive stuffed panda I should have got her at the start, and when I gave it to her she was so happy she cried.

'I'm not crying because it's a panda,' she said when I led her into her room and showed her what was there. 'I'm crying because it's from you.'

And that just left Mum.

Well, Mum and one other special person.

Most of the money went into buying back Mum's dodgy old camper van. Then we had to get the mechanic at number fourteen to fix it up and paint it sky blue (Mum's favourite colour). Now the van had a serving hatch, plus cupboards in the back, and a big gas stove for boiling spaghetti.

We got the artist at number twenty-two to write THE SPAGHETTI EXPRESS on top in bright pink letters.

It looked *magnificent*.

'Oh, Joe, I love it,' says Mum, holding her hands up to her face, like she wanted to keep her words in her mouth until she found the right ones. 'But what are we doing? All I do is put three drops of hot sauce into each dish! Is anyone going to want that?'

'Well,' I say, 'they are if you have the right sauce.'

And that's when Nico turns up, carrying as many giant tubs of Nico's Special Sauce in his hands as he can manage.

Nico works with Mum now.

He makes his sauce – the best sauce in Didcot, remember – and Mum adds her special touch. The thing that makes it not just sauce. The thing that makes it

Mum's sauce too. Three dots of chilli, and some love.

They drive the Spaghetti Express all over town together. Soon they're hoping to get a second van and expand into meatballs.

I don't think I will end up working in an office. I think I'm going to end up working with Mum. Darren and Joe 2 say they want Saturday jobs too, and they ask me about it every time we hang out together in the park.

Anyway, that night, people were lining up right the way down my street to get their spaghetti.

And everyone – even Darren Harper's mum and dad and that woman at number twenty – agreed that it was anything but average.

CHAPTER TWENTY-SIX

So I know this seems like a very long school project to hand in.

I did mention this was my school project, didn't I? It wasn't supposed to be. And I know I was only supposed to write about what makes THE MODERN FAMILY and how an average family would compare to one in the past, but once I started I couldn't stop. You probably wanted me to just hand in a few pages with a black-and-white picture of some serious-looking dudes washing a baby in a barrel and then saying, 'We have the jacuzzi nowadays.'

But my family is a modern family. A typical, normal, everyday, *average* family.

Except that, really, there is nothing average about us at all.

My sister is special. Sure, she talks a lot about pandas, but she is kind, maybe the kindest person I know, and just by being herself she has taught me to be kinder and nicer.

My dad was in a band called Samurai! Was your dad in a band called Samurai!?

And my mum? She makes the best mean Bolognese in town. And I know I'm supposed to say that because everyone thinks their mum does. But I've been to loads of people's houses and I love my mum's the most.

I suppose my point is that, all through time, every family has thought they were normal. I bet even the first cave family probably felt a bit average now and again. I bet they sometimes got sick of eating Dad's burnt mammoth every night, or having to go hunting and gathering every single day of the week, including Sundays. I bet they all thought the cave next door was much more interesting than theirs.

But there's no such thing as a totally normal family. We've all got something weird, strange and unique about us. Something that when we grow up, and tell other people about our childhood, makes them say, 'I'm sorry, your family did WHAT at Christmas?' or, 'Your family called it a WHAT?'

They say being special means being out of the ordinary.

But what's the thing that links my ordinary family to your ordinary family to everybody else's ordinary family?

It's that, however ordinary we are, we are each of us so very special.

And that's what makes a modern family.

And that's why I'm the luckiest kid in the world.

MODERN FAMILY ↗

By Joe Smith

Age 10

The End

Acknowledgements

I'm a lucky author, because the great Gemma Correll illustrated this book perfectly, so I'd like to thank her, as well as everyone at Simon & Schuster and in particular:

Ali Dougal! Rachel Denwood! Lucy Pearse! Laura Hough! Dani Wilson! Eve Wersocki-Morris! Clare Mills! Jesse Green! Lowri Ribbons! Katie Lawrence! Each one worthy of an exclamation mark.

My thanks also to Robert Kirby, and the kids who get to read these stories first: Elliot, Clover and Kit.

And thank you of course to YOU!

DANNY WALLACE is an award-winning writer and radio presenter who's done lots of silly things. He's been a character in a video game, made a TV show about monkeys, and even started his own country. He has written lots of bestselling books including *Hamish and the Worldstoppers* and *The Day the Screens Went Blank*.

GEMMA CORRELL is a writer, illustrator and cartoonist. In the past decade, she's collaborated with various companies to design over 400 products, co-host multiple events, and launch a magazine. Be sure to check out Gemma Correll on Instagram and her website gemmacorrell.com